Clint Had Dais...
Broad S...

His deep, warm voice lull... ...hummed to the baby. The tune sounded like a combination of 'Baa-baa Black Sheep' and 'New York, New York.' Jessie couldn't quite make it out, but that made no difference. He was quite a sight. So handsome and strong, so intoxicatingly masculine, and yet so gentle and tender to the precious package in his arms.

Jessie allowed herself to fantasize for just an instant that all her wishes had come true. She had woken up to the kind of Christmas morning she had dreamed about—both Daisy and Clint belonged to her...

And she belonged to them.

Dear Reader,

Merry Christmas from all of us at Silhouette Desire®! To celebrate, we've got an extra special line-up for you to enjoy over the holiday season.

We begin with Jackie Merritt's MAN OF THE MONTH, *Montana Christmas*, which is the conclusion of her spectacular MADE IN MONTANA series. Then Scarlett Morgan gets a lot more than she bargained for from her new business partner Colin Slater in *A Bride for Crimson Falls*, which is the third title in Cindy Gerard's mini-series NORTHERN LIGHTS BRIDES.

Gabriel's Bride by Suzannah Davis is a classic—and sensuous—love story you're sure to enjoy, and Anne Eames demonstrates a delightful writing style in *Christmas Elopement*. *Love-Child* by Metsy Hingle is a wonderful tale about reunited lovers, and Kate Little's *Jingle Bell Baby* will make you feel all the warmth and goodwill of the holiday season.

Have a fantastic time!

The Editors

Jingle Bell Baby
KATE LITTLE

*Silhouette, Silhouette Desire and Colophon
are registered trademarks of Harlequin Books S.A.,
used under licence.*

*First published in Great Britain 1997
Silhouette Books, Eton House, 18-24 Paradise Road,
Richmond, Surrey TW9 1SR*

© Anne Canadeo 1996

ISBN 0 373 76043 4

22-9712

*Printed and bound in Great Britain
by Mackays of Chatham PLC, Chatham*

KATE LITTLE

claims to have a lot of experience with romance—'The *fictional* kind, that is,' she is quick to clarify. She has been both an author and an editor of romantic fiction for over fifteen years. She believes that a good romance will make the reader experience all the tension, thrills and agony of falling madly, deeply and wildly in love. She enjoys watching the characters in her books go crazy for each other, but hates to see the blissful couples disappear when it's time for them to live happily ever after. In addition to writing romance novels, Kate also writes fiction and nonfiction for young adults. She lives in Brooklyn with her husband and daughter.

To Spencer, my 'real life' romance hero
and to our precious 'Kate Little.'

One

Jessica yanked another tissue from the box on her desk, dabbed her eyes, then soundly smacked the side of the old portable TV to clear the static. She didn't know why she kept watching this darn old movie. It must have been the fifth time since Thanksgiving and it still made her weepy. A person would think a person spending Christmas Eve alone would know better.

"Bet I could lip synch the entire script by now," she muttered. "Bells ring. Angels get their wings. Everyone in Bedford Falls lives happily ever after...."

On the small screen a young, smooth-cheeked Jimmy Stewart swooped his daughter up with one arm and with his other, hugged his adoring wife. All around them, a circle of friends and family smiled and sighed, radiating love and holiday cheer.

Jessica sniffed into a tissue as the theme music rose up and the happy scene faded.

The picture suddenly changed to a commercial, a homespun production featuring a local used-car dealer dressed as Santa, ho-hoing his way around a snowy car lot.

As Jessica snapped off the set, she heard the bells on the entrance to the café jingle, announcing the arrival of a late customer.

A very late customer. And the only one so far tonight. She wiped her eyes with another tissue and quickly smoothed back her hair. A few reddish gold curls escaped from her lopsided, upswept hairdo and she pushed them behind her ears.

Whoever was stopping by so late had better be satisfied with nothing more than coffee. Make that coffee to go. She didn't have the energy to start messing up the kitchen, not at midnight, when she should have flipped the Closed sign in the window an hour ago. And she would have, too, if that ridiculous movie hadn't distracted her. And if she'd had somewhere to go tonight, or someone to go to....

"Be right with you—" she called out as she left the small room that doubled as the café's storeroom and office. She walked briskly through the big kitchen and pushed through the swinging doors into the seating area, grabbing the coffeepot en route in a gesture that had become total reflex.

She glanced around, all set to explain that the menu was extremely limited. But the dining area, gaily decorated with lights and pine garlands, was empty. She looked around twice to make sure. Whoever had come in had left. Maybe over the TV she hadn't heard them enter, and the bells had signaled their exit?

Then she saw it—a large wicker laundry basket sat smack in the middle of the counter. Right between the cash register and a stainless-steel napkin dispenser. A plaid woolen blanket stuck out of the top. What in the world— was this some kind of joke? Jessica put the coffeepot on the counter and looked around the dining area again, this time peering in the wooden phone booth and then out through the front window at Hope Springs' desolate Main Street.

The snow that had started hours ago now fell fast and thick. The town's Main Street, with its old-fashioned storefronts, holiday decorations and cast-iron street-lights, looked like a scene that had been lifted right off a Christmas card.

"Not a creature was stirring," she whispered to herself, turning back to look at the basket. "Not even a—"

Her breath caught in her throat as a small white hand popped up from the blanket. She blinked and shook her head. Then, just as unbelievably, a small bare foot emerged, as well. Hypnotized, Jessica watched as the tiny hand swatted the air, grabbed for the foot and finally caught it. Then a sound, an unmistakable baby gurgle of satisfaction, followed.

With her heart pounding wildly in her chest, Jessica ran over to the basket and swiftly flipped the blanket aside. A bit of powdery snow that had collected in the folds sprinkled down to the floor.

"Oh my Lord!" Jessie said out loud.

A baby stared up at her, looking serious and wide-eyed, still clutching its foot in one hand. Not quite believing that the infant was real, Jessica reached out and ran one fingertip gently along the baby's smooth pink cheek. The baby tilted its chin against its chest, looking as if it might burst out crying. Then suddenly the baby smiled and clutched Jessie's finger in a sticky grip.

"Oh, sweetheart," Jessie cooed. The baby's smile widened in response.

The baby appeared to be wrapped in about three flannel receiving blankets that were now bunched around its middle. Jessica worked her way through the blankets and found that the baby was dressed in nothing more than a thin and stained pink-and-white nightgown. She reached into the basket and pulled the baby out, holding its small warm body close to her chest. "Where did you come from, little angel? Huh?"

The baby put a fist in its mouth, then rested its head against Jessica's shoulder. Golden curls rubbed against her cheek and Jessie thought she'd never felt anything so soft and fine. A mixture of baby lotion, formula and some other subtle, elusive perfume mingled in a scent that was distinctly baby. Jessica took a rich, intoxicating lungful and felt her heart clutch. Yes, there was indeed a lump of genuine, delectable babyhood in her arms. Pink and white and sweet as spun sugar. A lamb. A dove. A real live baby. Holding the baby to her chest in a firm but gentle embrace, she rocked from side to side, quieting the baby's soft whimpers.

"You're okay, kid. You're okay with me, little sweet potato," Jessie whispered.

The blankets had been dragged out of the basket and now Jessica could see that under the cushy bed the basket held some baby clothes, a number of disposable diapers and a plastic bottle.

A scrap of paper taped to the basket caught her eye and she pulled it off. It was a note written on a piece of white writing paper, folded in half and addressed on the outside "To Whoever Finds This Baby." Jessica sat down on one of the counter stools and propped the baby in the crook of her arm so she could read the note.

The handwriting was plain printing, clear and neat.

Please look after my baby. Her name is Daisy and she
is real sweet. I can't take care of her no more. I just
can't do it. Help her find a good home with people
who love her and can buy her things, etc. I am sorry.

Jessie dropped the note on the counter and turned to
look at the baby again. "Daisy," she said out loud, smiling at the baby. The name suited her, with her big brown
eyes, bright smile and halo of golden hair. "Hello, Daisy
sweetheart. Hello, little girl. You must be hungry, I'll bet.
You poor little thing. You poor sweetheart."

Daisy stared up at Jessica, wide-eyed and attentive.
Jessie laughed at her. Then, without a second's warning,
the baby burst out crying.

"Oh, golly—oh, my." Jessie bounced the little girl in
her arms, not quite sure of what to do next. "Oh, now,
sweetheart, please don't cry. What's the matter, honey?
What is it, sweet?" she asked the baby. "Does something
hurt? Are you sick?" The baby paused for a second and
stared at her, taking in a lungful of air, then exhaled,
screaming even louder.

Jessie willed herself to keep calm. Though she adored
children and desperately wanted her own, the truth of the
matter was that Jessie had little hands-on experience with
kids, and no experience at all in caring for a small baby.

"Uh, let's see now. What could it be? Maybe your diaper is wet. Is that it?" Jessica stuck a finger under the
edge of the baby's diaper and felt around. It felt perfectly dry. No luck there.

The baby's cries were rising, becoming sharper and
louder. "Okay, let's see," Jessie said out loud. "You must
be hungry then. That must be it."

The baby's cries continued. Well, there's only one way to find out if I'm on the right track. This little muffin sure can't tell me, Jessie thought.

"Let's fix you something to eat, Daisy. How about a nice bottle of milk? It might just be tonight's special," Jessie said as she whisked the baby back in her basket and, carrying it, headed for the kitchen.

Jessie set Daisy's basket down on the big butcher-block table in the center of the kitchen. Then she held Daisy while she rummaged through the basket to find the bottle.

The ride from the dining room to the kitchen had temporarily quieted the baby. But now Daisy started to make small fretting sounds again, which Jessica guessed would soon build into a full-fledged wail. She hurried around the kitchen, grabbed a container of milk out of the refrigerator and began to fill the bottle. But how much should Daisy get? She had no idea. She filled the bottle to the top, figuring the little girl might be real hungry. But shouldn't it be warmed up a little? Yes, that was right. You were supposed to warm it, Jessie decided. She took the bottle, emptied the contents into a pot and put in on the stove to warm.

Daisy was crying at the top of her lungs. Just about rattling the pots that were hanging over the stove, Jessie noticed. She tried to soothe her by rocking her basket, then picked her up and held her close and did a few laps around the butcher-block table, but to no avail.

"Your order is coming right up, ma'am. One bottle, room temperature. Sorry for the delay. Just happens to be the cook's night off and the kitchen is a bit backed up," she chattered to the baby in a bright, waitressy voice.

The baby stared at her. Her crying lessened to a soft whimper.

"We make a wonderful bottle of warm milk here, if I might say so myself," Jessie continued. "Babies come from miles around for our bottles and I think you will truly enjoy it, ma'am."

Finally the bottle seemed warm enough. Jessie placed Daisy back in her basket, then took bottle and baby back out to the dining room where she could sit down comfortably.

With Daisy settled in the crook of her arm, Jessica offered her the bottle. The baby clamped on and sucked with astounding force.

"This one is on the house, honey. And do let me know if there's anything else I can bring you—"

Daisy's face soon glazed over with a look of utter contentment. With her eyes half-closed, she reached up and held onto the bottle. Her little fingers rested trustingly on Jessie's and Jessie gazed down at the tiny hand, feeling a strange and wonderful thrill. A little milk dribbled down Daisy's chin and Jessie quickly wiped it away with a paper napkin.

She was just so darn cute, Jessie thought. How in the world had anyone had the heart to leave her?

While Daisy sucked away, Jessie guessed that calling the police and reporting she'd found a baby should be the next order of business. But then they would come and take Daisy away—wouldn't they?

The bells on the door jingled again and Jessie quickly looked up. Drat, she'd forgotten to lock the door and turn the sign. Well, she'd just have to tell whoever it was that she was closed.

A man entered. A huge, snow-covered man who stood with his head bowed, cursing softly to himself as he shook the white powder from his thick dark hair and stomped his heavy boots. The gesture and the sheer size of him distracted Jessica from the baby for a moment.

"Sorry, but we're closed," Jessica shouted in his direction. "You can have a cup of coffee to go, but I have to warn you, it's been sitting there all night and must taste like mud," she added, looking up at him again.

He had finally picked up his head and stared at her with brilliant blue eyes, eyes the color of a cloudless summer sky. The expression on his face, however, was anything but cloudless—it could only be described as a dark scowl. His dark brown hair, wet and slicked back from his forehead, accentuated his bold features—a wide brow, high cheekbones and square jaw. He was in need of a shave, she noticed, and looked as if he'd had a hard night that wasn't going to end anytime soon. But he was definitely one hell of a good-looking man. If you liked them tall, dark and difficult, that was. Which she certainly did not.

"Luckily I'm not here for the coffee," he curtly informed her.

"Well, the rest room is back and to the right," Jessie said, her attention still fixed on the baby. "Normally, it's for paying customers only, but I suppose on a night like this it can't be helped."

"And I didn't stop in to use the damn john," he said, sounding more than a bit insulted, she thought, at her assumption. "I came in to tell you to close up. There's a full-blown blizzard out there, lady, or haven't you noticed?"

"I guess I didn't," Jessie replied truthfully. She glanced out the window. Yes, it was snowing buckets, but as a native New Englander, the sight of a little—well, a respectable amount of—snow didn't throw her into a panic.

"Even if you're not concerned for yourself," he added in a disapproving tone, "you certainly ought to give a thought to your baby."

"Listen, you—whoever you are—" Jessica began, ready to set the stranger straight.

The baby had sucked the bottle down to the very last drop and now made a loud sucking sound on the nipple. Jessica turned her attention back to Daisy and gently pulled the nipple from her mouth.

"Now, wasn't that nice?" Jessie said to Daisy. "You were hungry, weren't you?"

Totally satiated, the baby stretched across Jessie's lap as floppy as a rag doll. Jessie wondered if she should just let her go to sleep. Wasn't there something else you were supposed to do?

Jessica rocked Daisy in her arms, trying to remember what it was you were supposed to do after babies ate.

"Aren't you going to burp her?" an annoying masculine voice asked. "She'll just wake up screaming with a gas bubble later."

That was it! They needed to be burped. Though grateful for the information, Jessie didn't thank him.

"Of course I'm going to burp her," Jessie said indignantly. She lifted Daisy up to her shoulder and began patting the baby's back, as she had seen it done.

Why did people make such a big deal out of taking care of a baby? There didn't seem to be all that much to it.

As she gave Daisy's back gentle pats, she turned back to the object of her ire, who had now come closer and was standing right over her. At close range he was even bigger, more imposing . . . and even better looking.

"Who the hell are you, anyway? Barging into my place, sticking your two cents where it definitely doesn't belong—"

"This is your place?"

"That's right. Jessica Malone, owner, manager, tonight's star waitress." She introduced herself, her tone edged with sarcasm.

He did not look the least bit mollified.

"Sorry, I'm new in town. I haven't gotten around to meeting all the local—" She could have sworn he was about to say "characters" but he caught himself just in time. "Business owners."

He smiled at her, not exactly a warm smile. Still, it did something wonderful to his face, Jessie couldn't help but notice, crinkling his eyes most attractively around the corners and causing an astoundingly deep dimple to crease one cheek. She would bet dollars to doughnuts—baked on the premises, of course—that this man didn't smile often. Not from the heart, anyway.

"Apology accepted," she said. "And you are—?"

"Clint Bradshaw, town's new sheriff." He flipped open one side of his jacket to show her his badge, pinned on a black crew-neck sweater that stretched across his muscular chest.

"Congratulations," Jessica said dryly. She felt her gaze fix on the man's rather impressive physique. He caught her looking and smiled again, just the hint of a grin at the edge of his well-formed lips that said, "Gotcha!"

She turned away, feeling the color rise hotly in her cheeks.

It was a classic, nonverbal, male-female exchange, one of the "taking inventory" variety. Not that Jessie had been taking inventory of all that many men lately. But at twenty-nine years old, with one broken engagement under her belt and a few more "definite almosts" on her record, she certainly knew the difference between looking at a man and *looking*.

She'd been caught *looking,* and now, at this very moment, she could feel Sheriff Clinton Bradshaw *looking* at her. She shifted in her seat, patting Daisy a little faster and feeling suddenly self-conscious.

All right, she knew she was a sight tonight, her outfit chosen for comfort, not high fashion. The pink waitress uniform was borrowed for the night from one of her employees, Ivy—who was ten years younger, ten pounds thinner and a good three inches shorter. It fit Jessica like a short, tight minidress. Beneath the short-sleeved dress she wore a red, long-sleeved thermal undershirt. But if that wasn't bad enough, Jessica had chosen to cover the damage with Aunt Claire's old gray wool vest. The hand-knitted vest, a most valued piece of her wardrobe, now looked like the ragged coat of an old dog, she knew, but she couldn't resist wearing it from time to time for purely sentimental reasons. Especially on a night like tonight, when she had felt so alone and down in the dumps.

Foreseeing the snow, she'd pulled on a pair of black tights and thick socks and her beat-up, clunky hiking boots that gave her legs a real Frankenstein look. Her long reddish gold hair had been swirled into a careless knot and secured with a large clip. The arrangement was now listing to one side of her head, the loose strands hanging in corkscrew curls.

Jessie unconsciously smoothed a few curls behind her ear as the moment of uncomfortable silence stretched on and she tried to think of something, anything, to say that would send this man on his merry way.

Daisy saved her, letting loose an amazingly loud burp.

Both of them stared wide-eyed at the baby for a moment, then Jessica started to laugh. She switched the baby from her shoulder to a sitting position on her lap. Daisy stared up at both of them, smiling and looking quite pleased with herself.

Clint didn't join in her laughter, Jessie noticed. But he smiled just enough to cause that devastating dimple to make another brief appearance. Jessie met his gaze for a moment and felt her toes curl inside her hiking boots.

"Look, the point is," he said, "I'd feel a whole lot better if you'd close up here and let me give you two a lift home. Your husband must be worried about you driving in this weather with a baby."

His tone suggested that any man worth his salt would not only be worried about the situation, he would be parked at the doorstep, waiting to escort the two of them home safe and sound in a snug little snowplow.

Jessica stood up and cradled Daisy's little head against her shoulder. The baby's prize-winning burp seemed to have worn her out completely. Though her eyes were wide-open, Jessie had the feeling that if she played her cards right, the baby would drop off to sleep in no time. Without another ear-splitting crying jag, she hoped.

She rocked the baby from side to side, mulling over her situation. She knew that sooner or later she had to officially report that she'd found an abandoned baby. And quite conveniently out of the blue, here was a suitable "official" to report it to. Yet, Sheriff Bradshaw had assumed that Daisy was her baby and her heart told her to just let Sheriff Bradshaw continue on with his assumption.

It wasn't as if she were telling him a lie; she just wasn't telling him . . . everything. If she did tell him the truth, it would only set the official wheels in motion and part her and Daisy all the sooner. Daisy sighed, snuggling closer. Jessica brushed her chin against the baby's unbelievably soft hair.

Couldn't it all wait until tomorrow? Or even the next day? her heart whispered.

But Jessica hadn't been raised that way. It was simply impossible for her to be anything less than completely and totally forthright. Although at times like tonight, she wished her nature would let her get away with just a little white lie here and there.

"No husband," Jessie succinctly informed him, "so I don't have to worry about anybody worrying."

"Oh." He looked down at his shoes for a moment, then back up at her. His expression was unreadable but his gaze was intense, making her lose track of her thoughts for a moment.

"Not only is there no husband, Sheriff, this isn't even my baby." Jessie took a breath and held Daisy a little closer in her arms. "I found her. That is, someone came in here a little while ago and left her. Right on the countertop in that laundry basket."

"Left her? Are you sure?" His thick brows came together in a frown.

Clearly the good sheriff was having a hard time believing that anyone could be so unconscionable as to abandon a helpless little baby.

"Is anyone *you* know in the habit of misplacing their baby?" Jessie asked him. "Here, look at this. It was attached to the basket."

Jessica picked up the note from the counter and handed it to him. His head bowed, he quickly read it.

"Well, I'll be damned." He let his hand drop to his side, still clutching the note. "Have you reported this to anyone yet?"

"Well, I'm reporting it right now, to you, I guess," Jessie told him.

He looked right into her eyes and for an instant she imagined that he had read every thought running through her head. I know you didn't *really* want to tell me about this baby, did you? she could almost hear him saying aloud.

"You'd better tell me the whole story, from the beginning."

"Well, let's see." She took a deep breath, deciding there were some details she'd just as soon edit out. Sobbing over that silly old movie, for one thing. "It was just about midnight, I guess. I was in the storeroom, catching up on some bookkeeping. The TV was on, too. I had just shut it off when I heard the bells on the front door ringing. Then I called out to whoever it was that I'd be right out—"

"There was no one else here?" he asked. Jessie nodded. "You don't run this place by yourself, do you?"

"I gave everyone time off for the holiday. I—" She caught herself starting to disclose some more personal details. "I decided to keep the place open anyway."

She didn't have to tell him everything about herself, did she? Yes, she was alone here because she had given Sophie, Ivy and Charlie the night off. They all had somewhere to go and she didn't. It was that simple.

Oh, she'd had invitations—more than she could remember refusing—from Sophie, who was making a huge dinner for her three children and eight grandchildren. From Charlie, who was going to his daughter's home in Maryland. From Ivy, who was going to spend the holidays with her folks who lived just outside of town. And of course, from Aunt Claire, who was on the first leg of a world tour and had tried to persuade Jessie to join her in the Greek Islands. Claire was spending the holidays exploring ancient ruins, then heading off for India.

Jessie always had invitations from the good people who worked for her and all her friends in town. But somehow, this year, she didn't feel like being part of someone else's celebration. She didn't feel like being the designated "favorite aunt," the close friend of the family who sat just outside the golden family circle, looking on hungrily at other's people's happy marriages and growing children. Christmas was a time for family, and Jessie didn't have one. And this year, she didn't feel up to the challenge of wearing a happy face while, inside, she felt so keenly the lack of all she was missing.

Now, did Sheriff Bradshaw need to know any of this?

Not on her life, Jessie decided. Daisy, who was resting with her head propped against Jessie's shoulder, gave a soft sigh. The baby felt relaxed and heavy, Jessie noticed, the milk in her belly taking effect.

"I think she's about to fall asleep," Jessie said, rocking slowly side to side.

Clint stared down at her solemnly and seemed suddenly lost in thought. Jessie was willing to wager that he wasn't thinking about her or even about the baby. No, he was miles away in some very private place, a place that wasn't a very happy one, either, Jessie would guess, for the expression that flashed across his face was one that Jessie could classify only as total emptiness. Sadness. Loss.

It transformed his strong features for an instant, then just as swiftly, it was gone and he looked at her again, wearing an expression that revealed no emotion at all.

"So you heard the door and came out here," he said in a low tone, mindful of the baby. "Then what?"

"There was no one here when I came out. I saw the laundry basket on the countertop, and then, after a moment or so, I realized what—or rather, who—was in it."

"And you didn't see anyone around, out on the street or getting into a car?"

"No, didn't see a soul." Jessie shook her head. "There was just that note."

Clint's gaze rested on the baby, who was fidgeting a little as she tried to fall asleep, burrowing her head into Jessie's shoulder.

"What kind of a mother would leave her little baby like that?" he asked, and the intensity in his blue eyes was frightening, Jessie thought.

"Oh, I don't know.... A young, scared, overwhelmed kind?" Jessie offered.

Maybe it was her Christmas spirit acting up, but Jessie didn't want to judge whoever had left Daisy and that note too harshly. At the very least, whoever it was had thought to bring her somewhere safe and warm.

Had they known that Jessie would be alone tonight in the café? Had they chosen her specially to find Daisy?

Jessie felt the baby's head drop against her shoulder and her breath go heavy and slow. "Are her eyes closed?" she whispered.

Clint stooped over to check. "Out like a light."

He lifted his big hand toward the baby's cheek, paused, then let his hand drop without actually touching her.

He straightened up and was all business again. "I suppose I'd better take her over to the hospital in White-wood."

"She doesn't seem sick," Jessie said. "She seems perfectly fine to me."

"It's routine procedure in a case like this. She needs to be examined and observed for twenty-four hours."

"But Whitewood is over an hour's drive, even in good weather," Jessie pointed out. "Do you really have to take her there tonight?"

He stooped over and peered at the baby again. "Regulations—besides, what else can I do with her? Wrap her up and slip her under someone's Christmas tree, maybe...."

His voice trailed off as he regarded Daisy's angelic expression.

"I'll take her," Jessie piped up, trying to control the eagerness in her voice. "She'll be just fine with me. I live only a few miles away and it will be safer driving her to my house than all the way over to Whitewood in this weather, don't you think?"

"I suppose—" Clint frowned, trying to weigh his official responsibilities against the flat-out convenience of Jessie's offer. The baby appeared to be perfectly healthy. There was no reason why she had to be rushed over to a hospital in a snowstorm. Which would certainly be putting the rules above consideration for the child's safety and comfort. And as for taking a chance on Jessica Malone, she certainly seemed to handle the baby with a gentle touch. And he could always make a few calls tonight to check her out. Everyone seemed to know everyone in this town. It shouldn't be too difficult to get a quick character check on Jessica Malone.

Clint considered himself a good judge of character; in his line of work he figured he had to be. He had made up his mind in about ten seconds about Jessie Malone. She was smart, stubborn and more than a little eccentric, he thought. For example, the way she was holed up all alone here, hiding out from the holiday.

But still unable to hide her good looks, he had to note, even in that getup, an outfit that made her look half chorus girl, half bag lady. When she'd stood up before and strolled around the place with the baby, he couldn't help but notice the enticing sweep of her long lean legs, her slim waist and soft full breasts. That mop of red hair looked as if it led a life of its own, and those huge brown eyes were lethal.

But no man in sight. Now, he found that curious. Maybe the "too damned independent for her own good" type? She had a story to tell, he'd wager. Still, something about her got to him, from the first moment he'd set eyes on her. Clint told himself he'd just been away from female company for too long. And he didn't plan on getting involved with any of the local citizens. Hell, he wasn't looking to get involved with anyone. Besides, just one glance at the way she was cradling and cooing to that baby should be warning enough for him to steer clear.

He raked his hand through his dark hair and finally met Jessie's questioning gaze. "You know how to take care of a baby, I guess, right?"

"Uh, sure I do. Nothing to it." Jessie casually shrugged, trying not to disturb Daisy. "I've taken care of loads of babies. Loads."

The sheriff met her gaze with his penetrating blue eyes and Jessie stared back at him, willing herself to look innocent and honest.

Okay, so she was lying a little. She was lying big-time, actually, but she just couldn't help herself. Besides, she and the baby were getting along just fine, weren't they? She'd already managed to feed her and burp her—with a little prompting—and had put her to sleep like a pro. As for diaper duty, she'd get to that in due time, she had no doubt. She could handle this, Jessie assured herself. For heaven's sake, it wasn't rocket science.

Besides, it would take a crowbar to pry the baby out of her arms. It felt so good holding her, Jessie thought, she wasn't about to give her up without a struggle.

"I guess you can take her home tonight," he said finally. "That seems the most sensible thing to do, under the circumstances."

"Can I really? That's just great," Jessie said in a hushed tone.

The radiant look on her lovely face nearly took his breath away. He pulled his gloves from his pocket just to supply some distraction.

"Like I said before, I'll drive you two home," he said. "Where do you live?"

"I've been driving in snow like this and worse my whole life. I won't have any problem," she assured him.

"Are you always so darn contrary, or is it just something about me?" he asked her in a curious tone. "Is it the badge? Some people have a real thing about authority, you know. It's not at all uncommon."

Jessica paused for a second. He was staring at her in a way that was downright unnerving. She nervously bit down on her lip. "I'm not sure, Sheriff," she ventured with a small, teasing grin. "Maybe it's your after-shave."

"I don't wear after-shave," he replied, the corner of his mouth tilted up in the hint of a smile—but he was fighting it all the way. "If you don't need a ride, I'll follow you. And I'll take the baby in my car. I need to make sure you get her home safely," he responded in a stern tone.

"Whatever you say," Jessie responded with a shrug.

She blew at an errant wisp of hair that was hanging down along the side of her cheek, tickling her nose. Before she could shift the baby around to reach it, Clint reached out and brushed it back behind her ear. His fingertips brushed soft as a whisper against her cheek, but the brief contact jolted her as if she'd been touched with the live end of an electric wire.

Their gazes met for one searing second; his eyes darkened and Jessie looked away.

"Uh, thanks," she mumbled.

He stepped back and cleared his throat. "I guess we'd better get out of here."

"Right," Jessie said. "I'll just wrap her up."

She carried Daisy to her basket and began to wrap blankets around her with shaky hands. What in the world was happening here? Was she getting all tangled up inside over this grim lawman?

Nonsense, she told herself. It was the snowy, silent night, and the sheer adventure of finding a baby—period, Jessie told herself.

"We're ready," Jessie said, slipping on her coat and scarf.

Clint took the basket from her and headed out to the car. As he walked along she could hear him talking softly to the baby, and she smiled. Jessie gave the café one last long look before closing the lights and locking up, and she felt suddenly hopeful and bright, as if one part of her life were ending and new one just about to begin.

But it didn't have one damn thing to do with Clint Bradshaw, she reminded herself.

And it wasn't going to, either.

Two

The snow was falling fast and deep as Jessie slowly drove the familiar route home. Her small white farmhouse was just a few miles outside of town but she had rarely recalled the ride taking so long. As she guided the Jeep over bumpy, snow-covered roads, she could see the police car's headlights shining steadily a short distance behind her. She thought of the baby, secure in her basket in the back seat of Clint's cruiser—and she thought of Clint—and tried to ignore the odd little glow inside her.

The Jeep fishtailed as she turned into the long driveway and she steered hard to avoid skidding into a pine tree. Finally the vehicle lurched to a stop, the front end sunk into a hip-high drift.

She sighed and rested her head on the steering wheel for just a second before turning off the engine. She would have to do some digging to get this heap on the road again, but right now she had more important business to tend to.

Jessie hopped out, then glanced back to the police car that had pulled up behind her. Clint was already reaching into the back seat for Daisy's basket. He was quickly at Jessie's side, his long legs gliding effortlessly through the deep snow.

"You go ahead and open the door," he said.

Jessie trekked up to the door and got it unlatched, Clint following close behind. He stumbled into the house, holding out the basket like a fullback coming over the fifty-yard line.

"This baby could sleep through a tornado," he said. "Where do you want her?"

"In the living room will be fine for now, I guess." Just behind him, Jessie peeked inside the basket as he carried it into the living room and set it down near the Christmas tree. Daisy was still, miraculously, sound asleep. Jessie reached in and arranged the blankets around her.

"Don't start fussing over her too much now—she'll wake up," Clint whispered as he crouched down next to her.

"Do you think she's okay in there? Maybe I should make a little bed for her from a dresser drawer or something," Jessie whispered back.

"She looks pretty snug as is. I wouldn't move her. You'll put her in your bedroom tonight, while you're sleeping, right?" he asked.

"Of course I will—" Jessie turned to him, wide-eyed and indignant. "As if I'd let this little girl sleep down here all by herself."

"All right. Just checking," he whispered back with a hint of laughter under his voice. "No more questions, promise. I know you'll take good care of her."

She would indeed. That was certainly no lie. She'd take the most excellent care of this baby, even if she had to stay up all night staring at her like a loyal watchdog. What she didn't know about baby care Jessie was determined to make up for in dedication.

"Tell me something, Jessie," he whispered. "When you got up this morning, did you ever think you'd find something like her under your tree?"

Jessie glanced at him, but made no answer. He had a teasing edge to his voice that Jessie would bet one didn't hear too often. She looked down at the baby again and made a tiny adjustment in Daisy's blanket.

"To tell you the truth, she's exactly what I asked Santa to bring me."

"You must have been a *very* good girl this year," he replied.

She gave him a questioning sidelong glance, then looked back at the baby. "What are you expecting in your stocking this year? A lump of coal, I'd bet."

"Sounds about right," he admitted with a nod. "But I do have my memories." His wicked grin made her heart skip a beat.

She smiled despite herself, but didn't dare stare into his eyes for too long.

"She's a miracle, isn't she?" Jessie said, turning the conversation back to the baby.

"She is, indeed." Clint nodded, his gaze moving from the baby back to Jessie. Had he done the wrong thing by letting her take this baby home, even for one night? The expression on her lovely face was enough to move even his old battered heart. How was it that she wasn't married with a houseful of kids of her own? This lady wanted a baby—a baby and all the trimmings. All the things that he could never give a woman.

And he had wondered why he was even thinking in that direction. It had to be the baby that had put him in this strange mood. He knew how a child, a sweet little baby girl like this one, could so easily steal your heart. And he knew the pain of losing one.

"Well, everything seems to be under control," he whispered. "I've got to go."

Abruptly he stood up. Jessie stood up, too, wondering about his abrupt change of mood. She had just been about to offer him coffee, but it was probably better that she hadn't, she decided. She had to admit that now that he was leaving, she felt just the tiniest bit nervous about being alone with the baby.

Get a grip, she urged herself. You can't admit now that you don't know beans about taking care of her.

Besides, it was probably better that he was leaving. This dark, strong, mercurial man genuinely unnerved her. Still, she wondered why, while half of her was willing him to go, the other half was already wondering when she'd see him again.

"So, what happens next?" Jessie asked as she followed him to the door.

"Someone will come by tomorrow and pick up the baby. I guess they'll call you in advance for directions and such. You'd better give me your number," he added and took a small pad and a pen out of his jacket pocket.

Jessie gave him the number, silently registering that the someone who would call and come for the baby wouldn't be Sheriff Bradshaw.

"Oh, and you'd better save all her blankets and the clothes that she's dressed in. We're going to need all of that for the investigation."

"Investigation?"

"We've got to try and find her mother, or whoever it was that wrote that note," he explained, sounding very much like an officer of the law, Jessie thought.

"But whoever left her doesn't want her. It says so right in the note," Jessie said. "Daisy wouldn't be returned to someone who doesn't want to take care of her, would she?"

The note of concern in her voice touched a nerve. The woman certainly had a point, but he sure as hell didn't make the rules.

"It will be up to the court to decide," he said simply. "That is, if we find her mother, or some other relative."

"And if you don't find anyone?"

"Then she'll be adopted. There are thousands of couples waiting to give a baby like that lots of love and a good home," he assured her.

Thousands of couples. The phrase echoed in Jessie's mind. Sometimes it seemed that the world was designed like Noah's ark; you couldn't get anywhere if you weren't traveling in a twosome.

"Yes, I guess there are," she said quietly. Then in a brighter tone, she added, "Just one more thing before you go, Sheriff—"

"Yes?" he answered sharply, pinning her with a definite "what is it *now?*" look.

"Merry Christmas," she answered.

"Right—Merry Christmas," he replied gruffly. "You've been a great help with this situation. Thanks."

"No thanks necessary," Jessie replied lightly. "Thanks for trusting me with her."

"Well, don't think I'm not going to check you out before the night is through," he warned her in a half-teasing tone.

"Oh?" Jessie's eyes widened. Then she laughed. "Well, let me know if you find out anything interesting. A woman likes to live up to her reputation."

He didn't answer. He just stood staring down at her for a long moment, his gaze floating over her hair and eyes, lingering on her mouth. Jessie felt something passing between them that was positively electric. He was going to lean down and kiss her. She felt as if she could barely breathe. Jessie looked up at him, meeting his gaze. Her lips parted. She held her breath....

But he didn't. He stepped back, and pulled open the door. "Good night," he said abruptly. And without waiting for her reply, he stepped out into the falling snow.

Jessie watched from the doorway as he walked down the path to his car and drove away. He was a puzzle, wasn't he? A tempting puzzle for a woman attracted by that kind of man.

But not her.

Not by a long shot.

She wasn't going to get her tail tied in a knot over Sheriff Clint Bradshaw. Not tonight, anyway. She had a baby to tend to and the very thought made her glow with excitement and shiver with flat-out fear.

This was a definite case of "watch out what you wish for because you just might get it," she reflected as she walked back to Daisy's basket. Well, it was just one night, she reminded herself, and the night was nearly over besides. Surely she could manage to care for one little tiny baby for a few hours? Why, the poor little girl would probably be asleep the entire time anyway.

It was almost as if Daisy had read Jessie's mind and had, on cue, decided to prove just how wrong a person could be about a baby. One moment, she was sleeping peacefully as Jessie looked on, contemplating how her tiny features were set in the most angelic expression. And a split second later, she was screaming at the top of her lungs, her body stretched with tension, her little face turning as red as a Christmas ball.

"Here we go again," Jessie mumbled, shaking her head as she reached for the baby. "Oh, now, now, sweetie. What's all this racket about, honey pie?" she asked the baby as she lifted her up.

It seemed unlikely that Daisy would be hungry so soon after having virtually inhaled that huge bottle, Jessie reasoned. It had to be something else. Her diaper! Yes, that was it. She hadn't given the downtown area any attention recently and was sure that must be the cause of Daisy's hysteria.

"Okay, sweetie. I think I have a clue now—" With the crying baby slung over her shoulder, Jessie scampered around the house, pulling open drawers and closets with her one free hand as she tried to fix up a makeshift diaper station.

She brought all the supplies into the living room and tossed them on the couch. Then she laid Daisy down on the couch on an open bath towel and got to work. Removing the dirty diaper and cleaning the baby's bottom was no problem. But the disposable diapers were not nearly so easy to use as they looked. Jessie found that securing one around a squirming, wailing infant was quite a challenge. Almost as fast as Jessie could get the diaper on her, Daisy seemed to twist and burst out of it, messing up all the sticky stuff on the tabs.

When Daisy was finally, though haphazardly, diapered to Jessica's satisfaction, the room was littered with clean but unusable failed attempts.

The baby's nightgown and undershirt were also wet, Jessie noticed while diapering her. After another long bout of squirming, crying and figuring out what seemed to Jessie a very complicated arrangement of snaps, Daisy had on a fresh diaper and a clean, dry undershirt and nightie.

Exhausted but proud, Jessie picked up Daisy and carried her back to her basket. Just as she was placing the baby back in her basket, however, she realized that somewhere during the clothes change, Daisy had managed to dirty her diaper again.

This time, in a more substantial manner.

"Courage, Malone," Jessica said, bolstering herself. "You can do it."

Daisy smiled up at her and stuck her fist in her mouth.

Jessica carried her back to the couch, and went through the entire operation one more time.

By the time Jessie had Daisy cleaned up again, the baby had begun a whimpering cry. Jessie realized that several hours had passed since she'd been fed. She fixed Daisy's bottle quickly and fed her.

She was careful this time to remember to burp the baby. As Daisy gave out another astounding burp, Jessie glanced at the clock. It was well after three. Didn't babies need to sleep a lot? Daisy seemed totally unaware of that part of her job description and did not look to Jessie at all likely to fall asleep anytime soon.

Jessie swaddled Daisy in a blanket and sat down with her in a rocker near the Christmas tree. The only lights in the room were the brightly colored tree lights, and through the large bay window Jessie could see the snow outside still falling.

In an hour or two, Christmas would be here, Jessie thought. As she rocked Daisy and hummed a lullaby, she thought back to the Christmas-morning rituals of her childhood. No matter how early she woke up, Aunt Claire had always gotten up just a little before her and there was a big mug of hot cocoa and a slice of her aunt's special cinnamon Christmas bread waiting at her place. And even though the bread and cocoa were delicious, Jessie couldn't sit still at the table long enough to eat them. With her mug and dish in hand, she'd dash into the living room and start unwrapping her presents as Aunt Claire looked on.

Jessie missed her aunt especially on the holiday. She could only dimly remember her parents, who died in a car accident when she was four years old. Claire, her father's older sister, had taken her in.

Claire had never married or had children of her own, and though she was well into middle age when Jessie arrived in her life, she was a wonderful, devoted parent. She had showered Jessie with love and had been there for her, to celebrate her successes and support her over the rough spots.

Not that there had been all that many rough spots, Jessie conceded. She'd just hit one great big one, on Christmas Day five years ago; a major pothole on the road of life that had spun her life around like a crash car in a demolition derby.

She was to marry Sam Kincaid, the boy she'd grown up with, the first boy she'd ever kissed, had ever flirted with, danced with, had ever made promises and plans with. But when the time had come for their marriage ceremony to begin, Jessie had waited at the church, dressed in her white satin gown, as her family and friends looked on. Even now she remembered thinking how lucky it was that the veil had been pulled over her face, concealing her distraught expression as she'd waited. And waited. And waited.

Finally the minister had taken her aside. Some flowers had been delivered for her. He'd led her to his office and had given her the bouquet. A letter had been attached, from Sam. It'd been full of regrets and apologies. But still, Sam didn't want to marry her. It wouldn't be fair, he'd explained, since he had fallen in love with someone else. That someone else being a woman who was willing and even eager to make a life in the city—in Boston, or maybe even New York. While he knew that Jessie would never willingly leave Hope Springs.

I am sorry for the pain I have caused you, Jessie, he'd written, *but I know someday you will look back and see that it has all turned out for the best.*

Well, five years to the day had passed and still that elusive "someday" had not arrived. Jessie wondered if it ever would. Oh, she had quickly learned that there was indeed life after Sam. She'd picked up her skirts and plowed on, as Aunt Claire would say, and had never wasted a moment feeling sorry for herself.

The time had passed. People finally stopped talking about her "disappointment." Year to year, her life changed. Aunt Claire decided she'd had enough New England winters for one lifetime and had retired to Arizona. She left Jessie the café and enough money to buy her own home.

In the past five years, Jessie had done her fair share of dating, yet she had never fallen in love again. Did you only get one chance for love and happiness? she sometimes wondered. Had her chance been used up on Sam Kincaid?

Maybe she was waiting in vain for something that didn't exist. Maybe she should just marry the next nice, acceptable man that came her way. Was there even such a thing as true love? She believed she had felt it for Sam and yet, their marriage had been so...expected. Expected by their parents and friends—by the whole town, actually. Thinking back, she couldn't even recall if Sam had actually proposed to her. Had she and Sam really loved each other—or were the feelings they shared more a mixture of familiarity, friendship and adolescent hormones?

Perhaps the only deep regret she had now about missing out on marriage was the fact that she wanted a baby— a baby just like sweet little Daisy, who was cuddled against her and not far from sleep.

Jessie glanced at the presents under her tree that her aunt and friends had sent her. The best gift of all this Christmas was Daisy, she realized, looking down again at the bundle in her arms. Daisy had finally fallen asleep, her head nestled against Jessie's breast. Jessie stared down at her in wonder. She knew now what it was to hold an angel in her arms.

If only I could keep her, she thought. Keep her forever.

Daisy shifted in her sleep and Jessie wondered if she should get up and settle Daisy comfortably in her basket. But then she decided not to risk waking her so soon after she'd fallen asleep. Jessie closed her tired eyes and kept rocking.

Thump. Thump. Thump.

Jessie opened her eyes. Someone was banging on the door. She started to get up and her sleep-muddled mind wondered for a second why she had fallen asleep in the rocker. Her body ached—especially her arms—and she realized in a flash that the strange weight in her arms was a sleeping baby.

Jessie's eyes fully opened and it all came back to her. She had fallen asleep in the rocker with Daisy. She wondered what time it was. The living room was dark, but not nighttime dark. She glanced out the window and realized that the snow was still falling.

The thumping had stopped for a moment, but now started again in earnest. Daisy was squirming, but not quite awake. Jessie got up from the chair with the sleepy baby cuddled against her shoulder.

Jessie trudged to the door and pulled it open. She felt a knot instantly clench up in her stomach.

"Looks like I woke you," Clint Bradshaw greeted her.

She hadn't been able to guess who was banging on her door. But he was the last person she'd expected to see. Was he here to take Daisy after all? So early?

"I guess you did." Jessie lifted a hand to her sleep-tousled hair. She couldn't imagine what she looked like. She didn't want to know. "We—uh, had a late night," she said. She pulled the door open wider and stepped aside. He came inside, his big body instantly filling up the small foyer and creating an uncomfortable sense of intimacy between them.

He stared down at her. "How's the baby?"

"Oh, she's fine." Jessie looked at the drowsy baby, then back up at Clint. "Still a little sleepy, I guess."

"Did she cry much last night?"

"A little," Jessie replied. "I guess she missed her mother."

Jessie could now recall falling asleep with Daisy in the chair the first time. Daisy waking, getting fed and changed and having another crying spell a few hours after that and Jessie ending up right back in the chair with her some-time right before dawn, only to fall asleep again.

"Yes, I guess so," he answered, nodding.

Enough of the small talk, Sheriff, she wanted to say. It's really not your style anyway.

"Have you come to take her?" Jessie forced herself to ask him.

He removed his hat and gloves. His expression showed no emotion. "Tired of her already?"

"No—no, not at all. She's not a bit of trouble," Jessie protested, some part of her mind registering that in some sense, her words weren't entirely true. The baby had been heaps of trouble and had kept her running all night long. But she wouldn't have traded those hours with Daisy for anything.

Clint looked down at her, his gaze narrowed. And though the look was clearly a suspicious one, Jessie couldn't help but notice the attractive little lines fanning out at the corners of his eyes. Damn, but the man was something to look at. Even more so in the light of day.

"Well, you can keep her here until tomorrow. Or maybe even the day after," Clint said. "Providing, of course, you want to."

"Two whole days?" Jessie felt her deflated heart fill with joy. "You mean it?"

"I guess that's a yes," Clint said dryly, the hint of a smile teasing the corner of his mouth.

"Of course it's a yes." Jessie smiled up at him. "But why? I thought you said someone would come for her today."

"The roads between here and Whitewood are a mess with the snow and the social services people at the hospital are all off for the holiday anyway," he explained. "Nobody seems to think that there's any emergency about bringing her in."

"Did you hear that, baby?" Jessie happily whispered to Daisy. "Maybe we'll get lucky and it will snow for a week."

"Yeah, well, it just might." Clint didn't seem to consider this a fortunate turn of events, Jessie noticed. "We'll see how you sound two days from now, snowed in with a tiny baby.''

"I wouldn't mind being snowed in with her for a month," Jessie replied.

Daisy, who was balanced on her hip, reached up and grabbed a long loose curl of Jessie's hair. She yanked it with surprising strength. "Ouch!" Jessie yelped and gently pried the baby's fingers free. "No, honey. Not the hair," Jessie said patiently.

Clint glanced down at her with an "I told you so" look, but she ignored him.

"I brought you some supplies," he said. "They're out in the car."

"Supplies?"

"Diapers, bottles, formula, rubber ducks. Hell, from what I've seen, babies need mountains of stuff," he said as he pulled on his gloves and hat again. "And you can't very well take her out in this weather," he added, his hand on the door. "She doesn't even have a snowsuit or a car seat."

"Uh, no, she doesn't. I guess you're right," she had to agree.

Snowsuits? Car seats? Jessie wondered how he had become so well-versed in the secret language of babies. Was he married with enough offspring to fill a minivan? He looked and acted single. And he didn't wear a wedding ring. But all that could be said of many men who were anything but unattached, Jessie reminded herself.

"I'll be right back," Clint said, swinging open the door. "Better keep her out of the cold draft."

"Oh, right. I'll leave the door unlatched," Jessie said, heading for the living room.

As Clint disappeared out into the snow again, Jessie dashed to her bedroom, hugging Daisy close. She set

Daisy on the bed and quickly changed her diaper. She had perfected her technique during the night and now managed to put a fresh diaper on the baby without using up half a bag of them in the process.

She was about to scoop Daisy up and take her back out to the living room when she caught sight of her own reflection in the mirror over her oak dressing table.

Jessie winced.

After bringing Daisy in last night, she hadn't had a moment to think about herself. Not even time enough to shower and change into her nightgown. She had slept in the rocking chair, wearing a big plaid bathrobe over her waitress uniform. Half the pins had fallen out of her hair and it now looked like something was nesting on her head.

Oh, Lordy! It was amazing the man didn't turn and run when I opened the door this morning, she thought. She was about to put Daisy down and attempt some emergency repairs when she heard an unholy roar from the living room.

"What in God's name—" It was Clint. She scooped up Daisy, then rushed down the hallway just in time to see Clint standing in the doorway of her living room with white parcels hanging from each hand.

She wondered what the problem was. Had he hurt himself? Twisted an ankle in the snow? She drew closer and stood right behind him. She looked past his broad back and through the doorway to see what he saw.

The living room looked like a cyclone had struck. Large, white balls of rejected diapers littered the couch and floor. Baby clothes, towels, all of Daisy's blankets, cotton balls and a few brightly colored plastic cups that Jessie had used to amuse the baby, covered every flat surface.

Just the fallout from her wild night with Daisy, but she hadn't had a chance to tidy up.

He turned to her, his expression dark, his gaze pinning her like a butterfly on a specimen tray.

"What the hell happened in there?"

"It...uh, got a little out of control last night with the baby, I guess," Jessie stammered. "She wasn't...um, quite as easy as I thought to take care of."

"You told me you knew all about taking care of a baby," he reminded her in a stern, quiet tone.

Jessie's mind raced. She could lie her way out of this. She could tell him that Daisy was a particularly difficult baby. The roughest, toughest, most stubborn little critter she'd ever come across. Though the baby's present calm disposition certainly belied that explanation.

"Well? Do you or don't you?" he demanded.

"It's just—" Jessie cleared her throat and started over. "It's just that it's been a while since I watched a baby alone and those darn disposable diapers must have been factory rejects because—"

Daisy reached up and swatted Jessie's mouth. The baby had obviously been entranced by the movement of her lips, but the gesture made Jessie think she was trying to say, "Cut the bull, Jessie. This guy isn't buying."

Jessie paused and looked down at Daisy. She took her little hand and pressed a soft kiss on the baby's palm. Daisy gurgled and smiled.

"You don't really have much experience caring for kids, do you?" he asked again, in a softer tone.

"Uh, no." Jessie glanced up him, then down at Daisy again. "No, I don't," she admitted with a sigh. "But I must say I got a crash course last night."

"It sure as hell looks like something crashed in there," Clint said, glancing into the living room again. "Crashed and burned."

Jessie studied his expression. The elation she'd felt hearing that Daisy was staying for the next two days instantly drained away.

She walked past him into the living room and sat down in the rocker. She sat Daisy on her lap and rocked. The baby's eyes widened and she smiled as the chair dipped to and fro.

"I guess that means you don't want to leave her with me after all," Jessie said with her gaze still fixed on Daisy.

Clint was standing near the chair, looking down at the two of them. He pulled off his gloves, then removed his jacket and placed it on a chair. He sighed and rubbed his face with his hand.

"I don't know that I have much of a choice," he finally replied.

Jessie looked up at him. She could feel her gaze getting misty, her eyes filling with tears. This was so silly. She knew the baby had to go sooner or later. Today or the day after next. What did it matter? And she had lied to him. She could no longer deny it.

She sniffed and looked down at Daisy again. She didn't want to cry. At least not in front of him.

Daisy was happily amusing herself with Jessie's fingers. She let out a happy, high-pitched shriek that shattered the tense silence.

"What now?" Jessie asked him in a thick voice.

He ran a hand absently through his thick hair. A muscle twitched in his lean cheek, yet his expression showed nothing. Not anger or even annoyance. Certainly not sympathy.

"I guess I'll have to take her back," he said.

And the look on her face just about broke his heart. Those huge brown eyes, glistening with unshed tears. Her head bowed again as she stared down at the baby who sat so contentedly in her lap. She looked as if she'd run herself ragged last night, he noted. Without a word of complaint, either. He had the craziest urge to lean over and wrap his arms around her, to feel her head rest on his shoulder as some of that wild, wonderful hair brushed against his cheek.

You are ten kinds of a fool, Clint silently cussed himself. He should have known better than to get involved with this woman—he should have known a hell of lot better by now.

Jessie cleared her throat and looked up at him. "You seem to know a lot about babies," she remarked in a quiet voice. "What to do for them and everything."

His eyes narrowed. His expression hardened. "I'm not able to care for Daisy, if that's what you're driving at. For one thing, there's no one to stay with her when I'm on my shift, or called out for an emergency."

All he'd said was true and certainly logical. But there was something under his words, some other, more personal reason why caring for Daisy by himself was not an option—though he clearly knew how. Something in his past, Jessie guessed. She had the urge to probe further, yet something in the way Clint looked at her at that very moment warned her off. His look told her that she was treading on very sensitive ground and would do best to back off.

"Oh, I understand," Jessie said. "I wasn't suggesting that you could look after her. It's just that, I was think-

ing, since you do seem to know how to care for her so
much better than I do, that you could stay awhile and
show me what to do. You know, sort of give me some
baby lessons?''

Three

———

"You want *me* to give you baby lessons?" He stared at her; his thick dark brows rose and his blue eyes widened. "Are you this crazy all the time? Or is it just because of the baby?"

"Well, why not?" Jessie argued. She stood up, holding Daisy against her shoulder. "You could run through the basics with me for an hour or two. If you still don't think I can handle her after that, then you can take her to Whitewood and I promise I won't say a word."

Clint shook his head and tossed his hands up in the air. "I can take her right now, you know. I don't exactly need your permission," he reminded her. "And besides, you lied to me last night, Jessie."

Jessie stared at him and bit down on her lower lip. The way he'd said her name, as if they'd know each other for years, instead of hours, momentarily distracted her, his deep voice like rough velvet sweeping across her senses.

"Yes, that's true," she said quietly. "I'm sorry I did that. I apologize. It's not normally, well, something I do. But I thought I could handle her." Jessie looked down at Daisy, who was contentedly fingering a strand of her hair. "And I guess I just couldn't resist trying."

Clint drew in a deep breath. He was standing quite close to her, so close that she had to tip her head back to see his face. She was distracted by his nearness, yet didn't feel she wanted to—or was even able to—step away. His expression was unreadable; his well-formed mouth pursed in a frown.

"All right," he said finally. His voice was so low and deep, she'd hardly heard him. "I'll show you what to do. But if it doesn't work out, no arguments. Promise?"

"I promise," Jessie agreed eagerly. She could feel herself smiling so widely, it practically hurt. "I'll be good at this. You'll see."

The only thing he could see at that moment was a beautiful, warmhearted woman whose dejected expression had suddenly turned to pure joy. And now all that radiant loveliness was aimed right at him, shining just *for* him, and he felt as if he'd been hit by a zillion watts of sunshine. And appropriately enough, he thought wryly, he was melting at her feet, like a lump of something soft and sticky.

"Let's get started," he said gruffly. "I don't have a lot of time for this today." Although in truth, his shift didn't start until the evening.

He collected the bags of supplies he'd abruptly dropped in the hallway and carried them into Jessie's kitchen. Carrying Daisy, Jessie followed.

The first task on the agenda, Clint determined, was giving Daisy a bath. While providing a running, instructional commentary, he efficiently cleaned Jessie's kitchen sink and countertop. Then he set up the counter with a fresh towel and washcloth, bottles of baby shampoo, skin lotion and other essentials.

The tub was filled with lukewarm water and Daisy was gently submerged. Daisy looked too adorable for words in her bath, Jessie thought. She gazed up curiously at Clint and didn't even cry when he washed her hair.

"Some people like to rinse the baby's hair with a football hold," he told Jessie. At this point she knew that meant securing the baby under one arm, running-back style. "I prefer rinsing with a cup with one hand and shielding her eyes and ears with the other." He gently spread his big hand over Daisy's forehead as he rinsed the soap from her hair with a cup of warm water.

For the next two hours Jessie was an attentive student, even going so far as to take notes. She watched as Clint dried, diapered and dressed Daisy in a fresh outfit. He clipped her nails with a tiny nail clipper and swabbed out her ears with cotton balls. He sterilized baby bottles, prepared formula and put Daisy down for a nap with something he called the "walk the plank" method.

Jessie herself got a bit drowsy watching Clint pace up and down the same short distance of her living room. His deep warm voice lulled her as he hummed to the baby. The tune sounded like a combination of "Ba-ba Black Sheep" and "New York, New York." Jessie couldn't quite make it out, but that made no difference. With Daisy nestled on his broad shoulder, his dark head dipped as he hummed, he was quite a sight. So handsome and strong, so intoxicatingly masculine, and yet, so gentle and tender to the precious package in his arms. Jessie allowed herself to fantasize for just an instant that all her wishes had come true. She had woken up to the kind of Christmas morning she had dreamed about: both Daisy and Clint belonged to her... and she belonged to them.

"Jessie?" She heard Clint softly whisper her name. And the sound of his voice, calling her name so intimately, blended into a wonderful dream. A dream she didn't want to wake up from. She smiled and rubbed her cheek against the pillow, her eyes still closed.

"Hmmm." She sighed. "That was perfect...."

"Jessie?" he said again. He softly touched her shoulder. "Are you awake?"

Her eyes flew open. His face was very close to hers, his blue eyes fixed on her, his wonderful, sexy mouth twisted in the slightest hint of a grin. She realized in an instant that she must have fallen asleep while she watched Clint putting Daisy down for her nap.

"Oh, I'm sorry." She touched her hand to her forehead. Someone—Clint, of course—had tossed an afghan over her and she abruptly flung it off. "Was I asleep very long?"

"Only a few minutes. You must be beat after staying up with Daisy all night."

Clint had not moved from his position, crouched down next to the sofa. Jessie didn't move, either. She felt like a princess in a fairy tale who opens her eyes after sleeping a hundred years to meet the gaze of her true love—the prince who has, with a single kiss, broken the spell and released the princess from her prison of loneliness....

Jessie tossed her head to clear away that fanciful thought. Clint was not her prince, or anything near it. She only hoped he wasn't angry that she'd fallen asleep during the very baby lessons she'd begged him for.

He didn't look angry. Far from it, she mused. She saw something thrilling in his gaze, thrilling and frightening, too. It was the unmistakable look of clear, potent desire. This man wanted her—and the realization made every nerve ending in her body sing and her breath catch in the back of her throat. She had the strongest impulse to reach up and touch his lean cheek with her hand. To pull his head down and feel the pressure of his warm, firm mouth on hers.

"You were talking in your sleep," he whispered, moving even closer.

"I was?" Jessie answered. She knew full well that she had an awful habit of talking in her sleep. And now she remembered her dream—and blushed to think of it. "Did I, uh, say anything?"

"Uh-huh." He nodded slowly. His eyes were still lit by the same fire, his face an unreadable mask. "I couldn't quite make out what you were saying...but it didn't seem to be a nightmare."

"No—it wasn't a nightmare," she confessed. She looked away, feeling her cheeks flush with the recollection of her dream. Then she looked back up at him. Their gazes met for a split second—something elemental leapt between them, like a flash of heat lightning streaking across a midnight sky. She started to sit up. Clint moved, too. He leaned toward her and their lips met instantly in an explosive kiss.

His mouth moved over hers hungrily and Jessie gave herself over to the wonderful pressure of his lips on hers. As she would have guessed—or dreamed—there was nothing tentative or uncertain about Clint's kiss. He didn't test the waters, he dove in headfirst. And Jessie eagerly followed. Her mouth opened under his as she met and answered the powerful thrusts of his tongue.

Her hands wandered from his thick hair to his broad shoulders, and she rose into his embrace, wanting only to feel more of his warm, strong body pressed against hers.

Normally, Jessie was a calm, reasonable person, even a bit cautious when it came to men. But the pressure of Clint's mouth on hers—his very nearness—robbed her of all composure, all caution, all inhibition. She didn't think, she didn't question. She simply reacted and, like a match struck against a flint, her senses exploded with a dazzling burst of light and heat.

"You taste good. So damn good," he murmured huskily against her mouth. Jessie could only moan in answer before his lips continued their sensuous assault.

Without separating his mouth from hers, Clint moved up on the sofa and positioned himself next to her, twisting around so that his broad chest covered her own. Jessie sighed against his lips, feeling a hot wave of pure pleasure as his body fit snugly against her.

Clint's big hands framed her face, his fingers trailing from her cheek, down to the opening of her robe. He smoothly pulled down the front zipper of her waitress uniform and slipped his hand beneath the silky fabric of her bra to cup her breast. Her nipples had hardened to two aching points and the callus-roughed touch of his fingertips felt electric. A hot, molten wave of pleasure coursed through her limbs. She twisted her body around, aching to feel more of his caresses.

He had pushed back the sides of her dress and slipped the straps of her bra down her shoulders to totally free her breasts. Jessie felt the cool air on her skin for a split second, making her sensitive nipples pull even tighter. Kissing her deeply, Clint covered her breasts with his large warm hands, massaging her with masterful movements as his wide thumbs stroked the tip of each sensitive nub.

Jessie groaned with pleasure against his mouth, her head tossing from side to side.

Her head fell back, and his mouth moved along her smooth white throat.

"Jessie, you are beautiful," he whispered as his lips moved lower. His dark head dipped and he cupped her breasts together. His hot, wet tongue moved over her nipples, lathing first one and then the next with a sensuous friction designed to drive Jessie wild. White heat zipped along every nerve ending. She raised her chest higher, surrendering herself completely to his sensuous assault.

Her hands roamed restlessly over his body. She tugged his shirt loose from his jeans and slipped her hands beneath. With bold, sensuous strokes she sculpted and caressed the powerful muscles of his back and chest.

The more he gave her, the more she wanted. Wave upon wave of hot pleasure broke over her and a honeyed warmth deepened at the juncture of her thighs.

As Clint's lips continued to twist and lathe her nipples and breasts, Jessie shifted restlessly on the sofa. Her hands moved hungrily all over his body, kneading the length of his thighs and brushing across the hard ridge of his manhood that bulged against his jeans. Clint gripped her tightly and she thrilled as she felt a hard shudder move through him. She wanted to touch him, to push him over the edge with pleasure, just as he was pushing her.

When had she ever reacted like this to a man? Not even in her wildest dreams. But this was no dream. It was better than any fantasy. Breathless, and aroused into a fevered pitch, she wondered how much more of this she could take.

Then, as if through a gauzy cocoon, Jessie heard Daisy's sharp-pitched cry. Clint heard it, too. He raised his head and took a deep, calming breath. Jessie shifted and quickly zipped up the top front of her dress.

"I'll get her," she said. She sat up and pushed her hair back.

"That's okay." Clint sat up and ran his hand through his hair. "I can get her. She's probably ready for another bottle," he added, glancing at his watch. "I'll get it for her."

"I think I'll go and change my clothes," Jessie said. She quickly sat up and swung her feet down so that they touched the floor. She felt as if she'd just jumped out of an airplane. Without a parachute.

Clint, on the other hand, looked cool and collected. He didn't seem affected one bit by their passionate encounter. In fact, if Jessie hadn't known better, she could have easily been persuaded that she had indeed dreamed the entire incident.

"Take your time," he said. Daisy let out another, more urgent squawk and Clint strode off in answer to her call. Jessie headed for the stairs on legs that felt a bit shaky. Yes, a shower—as cold as she could stand it—was definitely in order.

The cold shower had just the effect she'd longed for. It cleared her head and restored her sanity. And as Jessie dried off and dressed, she wondered if she'd made a first-class, giant-size fool of herself by responding so wantonly to Clint's touch. She felt a surge of warmth just recalling the scene.

Well, what was done was done. If her behavior had been out of line, then so had his advances. And if he was going to act as if nothing at all had happened between them, then she'd do the same. She would show Sheriff Bradshaw just how cool and nonplussed she could be. He'd probably leave as soon as she came downstairs to take over with Daisy, so it shouldn't be too hard to maintain the act.

Jessie dressed in her favorite worn jeans, a thick, bright blue turtleneck and short brown leather boots. She brushed her hair back in a ponytail and secured it with a clip. She stared at herself in the mirror a second, then grudgingly added a dash of cinnamon lip gloss.

High-pitched baby chirps and deep, masculine murmurs led her to the sight of Clint and Daisy playing in the living room. Clint had set up a blanket on the floor where Daisy laid on her back and was batting and kicking at the colored plastic cup and a few baby toys Clint waved over her. He had cleaned up the living room, Jessie quickly noticed. No trace remained of the scene of the crime. He'd also started a fire that burned brightly in the stone hearth.

He turned when he heard Jessie approach and his eyes moved over her with a quick, assessing glance. She gathered from his expression that he approved of her restored appearance.

"I can take over with Daisy now," Jessie said. She wanted to seem unruffled from his kiss, but she didn't want to sound rude. He had, after all, helped her out quite a bit this morning, and he was letting her keep Daisy.

"I'm not in that much of a hurry," he said without looking at her. "Come here. Look at this," he called, motioning her over to look at Daisy.

Clint supported Daisy in a sitting position, then stacked up the plastic cups in front of her. "Okay, killer, show 'em your stuff," he instructed her.

Daisy gazed around and sucked on her hand. She looked at the cups then back at Clint. "Go ahead," he gently urged her. "Show Jessie what you can do."

The baby waved her arms for a second, then reached out and knocked the tower of cups over with a quick swipe. Then she gurgled with laughter. Clint laughed, too. "Very good," he cheered. "Nice job, kid."

Jessie smiled and waved her hands. "Good work, Daisy! What a smart girl."

"Wait, watch this," Clint said. He grabbed a rattle, getting ready to show off Daisy's next trick. Jessie sat on the floor, too, on the other side of the baby. She reached out to support Daisy's back and her fingers brushed Clint's. A frisson of heat surged through her at the contact, but she forced herself to keep her gaze fixed on the baby.

Before long, almost an hour had passed. Daisy loved to play, and her attentive, appreciative audience—Jessie and Clint—was very resourceful in amusing her.

Finally Daisy stretched out on the blanket, swinging one hand at a toy and rubbing her eyes with the other. "I think she's sleepy," Jessie said.

"I guess her baby aerobics wore her out," Clint agreed in a soft voice. He grabbed a soft, flannel receiving blanket and showed Jessie how to wrap it around the baby on a diagonal, so that it would remain secure. By the time he had Daisy neatly bundled and had handed her back to Jessie, the little girl was just about asleep.

Jessie paced up and down the living room in front of the fire as she had seen Clint do a few hours ago. Daisy quickly fell asleep and Jessie placed her in her basket, fixing the covers so that she was snug as a bug.

"Well-done," Clint said when she turned to look at him.

"Thanks." Jessie smiled at him briefly. Now that the baby was no longer a mutual distraction, she suddenly felt self-conscious.

With his thick hair mussed from the baby's grabs and his blue eyes sparkling in the dancing light, he looked

pretty darn perfect lounging in front of the fire. So relaxed, so sexy, so vibrantly masculine. She imagined re-
turning to his side, stretching out beside him on the floor
and feeling his strong arms wrap around her once
more...and picking up where they had left off a few hours
ago....

Jessie abruptly turned her back to the sight and busied
herself adjusting an ornament on the tree.

Whoa—let's just slow down a second, pal, and take a
deep breath, she coached herself. You were going to play
it cool until he hit the road, remember? Why don't you
just give him a hint to get going so you don't get into any
more trouble?

"Well, I guess I'll be going," Clint announced, coming to his feet.

Jessie turned to him. "I was just going to fix myself
something to eat. Would you like to join me? If you're not
in too much of a hurry, I mean."

Now what have you gone and done! a little voice
shrieked at her. I thought you were going to get rid of him.
Oh, shush up, she silently answered.

He looked pleased by the invitation. Pleased and surprised.

"Sounds good. I'm not sure where I'd be able to grab
a bite on the road today. And you do own a restaurant,"
he added in a teasing tone, "so you must be a good cook."

"Well, don't get your hopes up," she warned him. "I
don't think I have much in the house. This is really going
to be a potluck special."

He watched Jessie as she headed for the kitchen. "I'm
not worried," he replied with a glimmer in his eyes. "So
far, today, my luck has been running pretty damn good."

And something in the way he said it sent a shiver over
her skin.

Jessie strode into the kitchen, pulled open the refrigerator door and surveyed its meager contents. She didn't know how to quit while she was ahead. That was her trouble. And now she had offered to cook a mishmash Christmas dinner for the most appealing and confounding man she had met in a long, long time. If she didn't watch out, she'd cook her own goose in the process.

"Can I give you a hand?" Clint had followed her into the kitchen and the sound of his voice right behind her gave her a start.

She straightened quickly, a bunch of scallions in one hand and a red pepper in the other.

"Uh, why don't you chop this?" she said, handing him the red pepper. She wasn't sure she'd be including the ingredient, but she thought it best to give him something to do. The thought of him sitting at the table watching her every move was unnerving. She'd be liable to dice off some important part of her anatomy.

He took the small wooden chopping board and knife Jessie offered him, and settled at the long oak table, largely out of her way. Jessie spread out her potential ingredients on the kitchen counter and tried to decide what she was cooking. A few moments later she was pulling down pans from the cast-iron pot rack that hung over the stove and pulling out mixing bowls and other tools of the trade from various cupboards and drawers.

"Have you lived in Hope Springs very long?" Clint asked her after a few moments.

"Practically all my life." Jessie briefly glanced at him over her shoulder. She told him how she had lost both her parents when she was a child and how her aunt Claire had raised her.

"Your aunt sounds like a special woman," Clint said.

"She is," Jessie assured him. "She retired to Arizona a few years ago and she seems to be having the time of her life, but I still miss her. She's globe-trotting with some friends from her retirement community. I haven't heard from her in about two weeks, but I think she must be somewhere in the Greek Islands by now."

"That sounds like some adventure," he said. "Have you ever wanted to leave here? See the world, I mean?"

"I love to travel," Jessie replied brightly. "I took a long, wonderful trip through Europe the summer after college. It was Aunt Claire's graduation gift. And there are still so many places I'd love to see," she added. "But I haven't had much time for vacations since I took over the café. I'll get to it someday though, I guess."

The truth was that, as much as Jessie loved to travel, the idea of taking off on exotic adventures alone seemed rather unappealing. She'd always imagined she'd be able to share those exciting experiences with someone she loved. Maybe it wasn't right to think that way. For all she knew, she'd be waiting for a traveling companion until she was old and gray.

"But you've never thought of living anyplace else?" Clint persisted curiously.

"I guess I've considered it." Jessie thought back to the time she had the impulse to follow Sam Kincaid to Boston, to make herself over into the city sophisticate he wanted, just to show him she could do it. Luckily she'd had better sense and more pride than to chase after him that way. "But something has always kept me here. I guess this town suits me." Jessie shrugged. "I couldn't imagine a nicer place to live."

Jessie turned back to the stove, wondering if he thought her hopelessly bucolic. Well, she couldn't help it. And she had no reason to apologize for it, either. She did love living in Hope Springs and had never seriously considered living anyplace else.

"How about you?" Jessie asked. "Have you moved around much?"

"All over the map," Clint answered. "My father's career in the army kept us moving. Let's see, there was California, Texas, Florida, Iowa, Oregon . . ." He shook his head. "You get the idea. We lost my mother when I was about thirteen. I guess it was hard for him, being left with three kids to raise all alone. But it seemed he needed to have a change of scenery even more frequently after that."

"So you have sisters and brothers?"

"One brother, a year younger. He's in California. And a little sister who's a doctor in Houston. She's got all the brains in the family."

And Clint got all the looks, it appeared to Jessie. Though she didn't make that observation aloud. "And where is your father? Still roaming around?"

"Still roaming. I guess he got so used to it that when he retired, he just couldn't stop. He bought himself an RV and just drives around the country, visiting old army buddies and long-lost relatives. When he wears out his welcome, he packs up and moves on."

"He sounds like quite a character," Jessie said.

"Oh, that he is." Clint laughed, a deep warm sound that made Jessie feel close to him.

"I guess moving around got into my blood, too," Clint added, looking up at her. "I can't seem to stay in one place for very long, either. I guess I'm just the restless type."

"I guess," she agreed. It was the sort of thing a man said when he wanted to give a woman a subtle warning, Jessie knew. Caution, slippery conditions ahead. Okay, she'd consider herself warned. The kiss they'd shared a few hours ago had rocked her to her very soul. But obviously it was not to be interpreted as the start of anything. She'd do well to remember that.

She glanced at him over her shoulder. Unfortunately, she liked the way he looked in her kitchen, his dark head bowed as he intently stared down at the red pepper. Staring at it with curiosity, he turned it first on one side, then on the other. Then he pointed it straight up and sliced it clumsily down the middle. Well, he wasn't much of a cook, that was for sure. Jessie turned away to hide her smile of amusement.

"You know, you can tell a lot about a woman from looking at her kitchen," he said suddenly.

"Oh?" Jessie laughed. "And what can you tell about me?"

Clint gazed around thoughtfully, taking in the room with a sweeping glance. The table was situated in front of three wide windows that were bare of curtains, but crossed by long wooden shelves that held colored glass bottles and pots of ivy and red blooming flowers he didn't know the name of. The long oak table that he sat at was surrounded by ladder-back chairs, and an oval-shaped rag rug underneath covered a bare wooden floor.

The stove was a huge stainless-steel restaurant model, the kind for a cook who meant business. The wooden cabinets were the old-fashioned kind, a warm, oak tone with glass panes that revealed a colorful collection of china and glassware.

This room was the heart of her house and revealed so much about her own heart, he thought. It was the kitchen of a woman who took in strays, made soup for sick friends and remembered birthdays. Hardworking and organized, but always with a thought for the feelings of others. Warm and sweet—but not without a certain fire.

She didn't do one-night stands. And she didn't play games. If she played at all, if was for keeps.

She was the type that could make a man—some man, not himself, of course—feel as if he truly belonged to something. Something larger than himself. As if he belonged somewhere very special—a place where a woman's tender heart was filled with loving thoughts for him alone, and bright-eyed children waited for their father to walk through the door. A very private place, from which he could see the future stretch out with some larger meaning, beyond his own pitiful start and end; a place where he could be a part of all that was good and right in the world.

He'd be a lucky son of a gun, that guy, whoever he was, Clint reflected. And why some man hadn't already claimed her was even a greater mystery to him.

"Well?" Jessie stared at him, waiting for his reply.

He cleared his throat and looked down at the half-chopped red pepper. "I'd say... I'd say, you're a woman who likes to cook," he answered blandly.

"Can't argue with that." Jessie laughed. "But I don't think you'd have much success as a fortune-teller, Clint."

"You don't think so?" he replied with mock disappointment. He rose and carried the chopping board over to where she stood. "How about a cook's helper?" he asked, glancing down at the pile of chopped pepper.

To Jessie's professional eye, the offering was a bona fide mess. She couldn't quite figure out how he had gotten the pieces of pepper cut in all different shapes and sizes. That couldn't have been easy. But she smiled and received it gratefully.

"I'd say you definitely... have potential."

"Thanks." He smiled, gracing her with just a glimpse of that sexy sparkle in his eyes. And he stood close to her, too close for her to even think clearly. Damn him, but even a mere look had a way of making her lose track of everything for a moment—where she was and what she was doing. His eyes seemed to say he felt she had potential, too. Potential for something she didn't dare to imagine.

"The food is almost ready," Jessie announced as she took off her apron. "I think I'll go check on Daisy," she said. "Then we can eat."

A short time later, Clint helped Jessie carry plates and flatware to the table and Jessie served their meal. She'd managed to find some mushrooms, scallions, bacon and cooked chicken, which she mixed with rice and spices, resulting in a savory-scented variation on jambalaya. Alongside, she served a tossed green salad and a loaf of hot, crusty bread.

When she served Clint his dish, he looked down at it curiously. Without saying a word, he took a bite. She watched his face carefully for his reaction. She realized that it was a regrettable unliberated impulse, but in spite of herself, she wanted him to like her cooking.

"Mmm, this is good," he said as he swallowed. He sounded as if he meant it, too.

"To the cook," Clint added, raising his coffee cup in a toast. Their gazes met and locked. Jessie felt her breath catch at the intense look in his eyes.

"You'll have to stop by the café sometime for a real meal," she said lightly. "Consider it my way of thanking you for helping me with Daisy today." Then Jessie looked down at her dinner and took a breath. "So, did I pass the course?" she asked hopefully.

"With flying colors," he said. "You're really good with children. A natural," he said thoughtfully. "How is it that you don't have a few of your own? If you don't mind my asking,'' he added politely.

It was a rather personal question, Jessie thought. Considering that they hardly knew each other. But sitting in her kitchen like this on a snowy afternoon, sharing a makeshift meal, Jessie felt as if she'd known him forever. And more importantly, as if she could be totally honest with him. Totally herself.

"Guess I'm just the old-fashioned type. Thought I'd wait for a husband before I got started on the kids.'' Jessie picked up her coffee and took a sip. "Of course, as time marches on, I have considered Plan B.''

"Plan B?'' he asked curiously.

"You know, go straight for the baby, do not pass Go. Single motherhood. Sperm-bank catalogs—'' She saw Clint choke slightly on his coffee at this last reference. "That sort of thing.''

"I get it.'' He nodded, covering his mouth with a napkin for an instant. Something had gone down the wrong pipe and now seemed to be tickling his throat.

"Are you okay?'' she asked solicitously. "Would you like a glass of water?'' She was secretly surprised that he was so easily shocked. She guessed he had some pretty old-fashioned ideas about such matters, too.

"I'm fine.'' He cleared his throat and sat up a bit straighter in his chair. He looked her directly in the eye. "Don't you think you're a little young to be considering sp—that, uh, type of thing?''

"I didn't say I was actually pursuing it. But this is a small town. Eligible men aren't exactly falling off the trees around here. Why, you're probably the first unattached, employed and ambulatory male under sixty-five to hit town in the past three years,'' Jessie wryly observed.

"Come to think of it, Clint, you're going to a popular guy around here. Better take some vitamins."

"I think I'm up to it," he replied dryly.

Jessie stared back at him. Her eyes widened, but she didn't dare say a word. She picked up her coffee cup to hide her smile. All she could picture was their romantic tussling on the couch that afternoon. He certainly had seemed . . . up to the challenge.

And with his looks, she imagined that the unattached female population of Hope Springs would be charging out to bag him like a field of English gentry riding out on a fox hunt. But she also had no doubt that this man could handle the onslaught of female attention.

"So you never got married because there's no one around here to marry, is that it?" he asked, abruptly turning the conversation back to her.

"No . . . not exactly." Rising, she picked up the dirty dishes and put them in the sink. "I was engaged once, but that didn't work out," she confided. "And I guess I've never met anyone since that I wanted to marry."

"I'm sorry." He pushed back his chair and looked up at her. "I guess I ask too many questions. A bad habit of being a police officer. I hope I haven't upset you?"

"Don't be silly," she said lightly. She took a pecan pie out of the oven, where it had been warming, and carried it back to the table. "It all happened about a hundred years ago," she added with a wry smile as she sliced into the pie.

He smiled back at her with a grateful expression. One that assured her that he really wasn't an insensitive oaf, asking a lot of personal questions about a lot of things that weren't really his business. No, he was genuinely curious about her. He wanted to know her. Maybe even as much as she wanted to know him.

She sat at her place and took a forkful of pie. "So now it's your turn," she said. "Why aren't you married with a truckload of kids? Never met the right woman? Or are you just too much of a rambling-type of guy and all that stuff?" she teased.

"I guess I'd have to check off all of the above," he answered in a quiet voice.

Jessie looked over at him. A slight change in his tone of voice had alerted her. Her question had definitely hit a sore spot. Not just the typical "none of your business" sore spot, either. No, this was something more serious, more painful.

While just moments before he had appeared relaxed and eager to dig into his pie, he suddenly looked as if something he'd eaten didn't agree with him. He set down his fork and sat back from the table.

Clint hated to lie to her, for a million reasons, really. The first of all being that he had pushed and prodded her into so many personal admissions and now, she'd asked one little question and he'd lost it. Of course she would assume from his answer that he had never married or had a family. He was deliberately misleading her. And something about her, in particular, made him feel doubly guilty.

But then again, something about her, about this house and simply sitting here, sharing a meal and their conversation, had gotten to him, causing him to feel things he hadn't felt in a long time. He wasn't at all sure if he liked it, either. And he knew that he just couldn't handle telling her about his marriage and everything that went along with that.

Not today. Maybe not ever.

"Gee—look at the time." Clint glanced at his watch. "I really have to go. My shift starts at five." He pushed his chair back and stood up. Jessie stood up, too.

"Is it that late already?" Jessie asked as she looked out the window. The little daylight that had filtered through the snowfall had all but faded away. She couldn't quite believe how fast the day had passed.

Moments later, Clint stood at the front door, fastening his jacket.

"If you need anything, or have any kind of emergency, just call me," he instructed, handing her a card with a lot of phone numbers. "Even if I'm out on the road, the dispatcher can reach me on the radio. Otherwise, I'll call later to see how things are going, all right?"

"Sure." Jessie nodded, secretly pleased that she'd be hearing from him again so soon. "Don't worry. I think we'll be fine."

He stared down at her. She brushed a strand of hair off her cheek and his gaze dropped down to her soft, luscious-looking mouth. Her lips were tilted up in just the hint of a smile. He wanted to kiss her in the worst way. He could actually taste it—a subtle flavor that was peculiarly her own.

Clint took a deep steadying breath. Lord, he was losing his mind today. He had to get out of this house and away from her.

And stay away, too. The damn woman was dangerous, he decided. Absolutely dangerous for a man like a himself.

Before he left, there was something that needed to be said between them. He'd been trying to find a way to say it all afternoon. Now seemed about as good a time as any.

"Look, before I go, I want to apologize for something—" he began.

"Apologize? For what?" Jessie stared at him curiously and took a step back.

"For, uh, well." This wasn't going to be easy, he realized, but he had to say it. "For what happened this morning...on your couch—" He gestured with his hat toward the living room.

"You're apologizing for kissing me?" Jessie stared at him with a shocked expression.

"I didn't come here this morning to make a pass at you is all I'm trying to say," he explained. "It just sort of...happened."

"Yes, it did sort of happen," she echoed sarcastically. "It sort of kept happening, too. As I recall."

"Well, I'm sorry is all I'm trying to say. I don't know what came over me. I never act like that—"

"Like you're attracted to a woman?" she asked in a curious tone.

"Of course I'm attracted to women. I'm attracted to women all the time—"

"But not me—that was the slipup that you're explaining here. Is that it?" she asked calmly.

"No! That's not it at all...." He slapped his hat down on his thigh and looked up at the ceiling, grumbling a low curse.

"Well, I'm not sure I understand. What are you trying to apologize for, Clint?" Jessie persisted.

He stared at her. What was happening here? Why did she have to look at him like that? She had crossed her arms over her chest and her pretty face was all puckered into a tight angry frown. All he was trying to do was apologize for jumping her bones—and set a few ground rules, so she wouldn't get her hopes up. Now she'd gotten him so turned around and tongue-tied, he was trying to convince her he liked women. And more to the point, that he liked her.

"Just forget it. Forget I ever mentioned it," he said, his hands upraised in a gesture of surrender.

"Well, so long," he said. "Take good care of that baby."

"I will," Jessie promised. He turned and pulled open the door. And as he walked out, Jessie heard him murmur something under his breath. It might have been goodbye, or see you. It might have been another growled expletive. She wasn't quite sure.

As Clint drove toward town his head was filled with thoughts of Jessie. The woman was dangerous, he decided. Definitely dangerous. The less he saw of her, the less time he spent in her infernal company, the better off he'd be.

He'd slipped up big-time by letting himself spend even a few hours with her. And that episode on her couch. Ouch. He'd behaved like a randy high school kid on his first date. Hell, what had come over him? He had more self-control than that, he chastised himself, even around a woman like her.

But now he had no excuses. He'd had his taste of her heavenly charms and he'd have to be satisfied with it. A blind man could see how it would go between them. He knew what type of woman she was and what she wanted from a man, and he didn't want any part of it. And he didn't want to hurt her. He had already been through that scenario too many times, as well. Well-meaning women who had put their heart and soul into proving that their tender affections could save him, revive that part of himself he'd lost when Emily died.

Well, it hadn't been their fault. It was him, something missing in him. Some essential part of his soul irretrievably lost. And he wasn't going to put himself through that futile exercise again, either. Not even with a woman as tempting as Jessie.

He would have relished kissing her some more. Kissing her...and everything else that might follow. He liked that little sound she made as she was melting against him, opening up to him. Lord, but he'd love to hear that sound some more. To savor all the little sighs and murmurs he could elicit from her if he ever had one night in her arms.

But he'd live without it. He'd have to. It wasn't the first time a woman like that had crossed his path and it wouldn't be the last.

He'd survive without Jessie Malone in his life. And she'd be a hell of lot better off without him.

No matter what she imagined.

Four

True to his word, Clint checked in by phone with Jessie late on Christmas night, early the next morning and then again in the evening. Their conversations were brief and limited to updates on the baby. Jessie found his distant, impersonal manner disconcerting. But when she factored in his apology for kissing her, it wasn't all that surprising.

He was trying to put distance between them, to diffuse any romantic notions he might have inspired by kissing her.

Being totally honest with herself, she felt hurt. Hurt and embarrassed. She'd had the impression that he liked her...*more* than liked her, even.

Perhaps it had been a mistake to practically fall into his lap—or rather, to welcome him so willingly into her arms when he had fallen into her lap. He must have decided she was some sort of man-hungry spinster. Especially after her little speech about the lack of eligible, able-bodied men under retirement age.

But it took two to make a mere kiss turn into so much more, so quickly.... It took two willing participants to practically make love the first time they got close enough to unfasten each other's clothing.

Well, she wasn't going to stay up nights, worrying about it, she promised herself. He was sending her a message: "Oops...never mind." Okay, she'd heard it loud and clear. And she'd take it to heart. He wouldn't be the first man who had scared himself silly by letting down his guard for a few hours. Let him run and hide. If he was that type, who needed him? Jessie told herself.

It was just about half-past nine, the day after Christmas and right after the third such call from Clint. Caring for Daisy had made for a very rewarding, but tiring day. Jessie had planned to read for a while and then get in a few solid hours of sleep before Daisy woke her for the night shift. But Jessie stretched out on her bed, totally ignoring her book as she puzzled over Clint.

Well, she certainly had better things to worry about, she realized. The snow had ended late on Christmas night and Clint had told her that the roads were now finally clear. It was fairly likely that he'd be taking Daisy to the hospital in Whitewood sometime tomorrow. Even though he hadn't been specific about when he'd come for the baby, Jessie had asked if she could come along for the ride to the hospital. He'd given her some curt, evasive answer that she had to interpret as a no.

Jessie glanced down at the baby, who was asleep in her basket right next to the bed. Lying on her back, with her two arms flung up toward her head, she looked like a little angel who had just tumbled down from a cloud. Jessie had the urge to kiss her soft cheek, but she didn't dare

wake her. She satisfied herself with stroking one of the
baby's silky blond curls with just her fingertip.

It was hard for Jessie to believe that she'd found Daisy
only two nights ago. It seemed much longer than that—it
seemed forever, when she considered how she felt about
the baby. How much she loved her. Was it possible to love
her in such a short time? Well, Jessie didn't care if it was
possible or not. She just knew that she did. She loved her
with all her heart.

And she couldn't imagine giving her up, handing her
over to some well-meaning, but impersonal group of
doctors and social workers.

She hadn't given Clint any hint of her feelings during
their phone calls. Even if she'd wanted to confide in him,
his cold, curt manner had been totally off-putting. Hardly
conducive to confessions of the heart, or to trying to win
him as an ally.

But an ally in what cause? she asked herself. Jessie
gulped and lightly touched the back of Daisy's little hand.
In the cause of finding out how to keep her.

Forever.

Yes, that was what she wanted to do. More than anything in the world, she wanted to keep Daisy.

Could she care for a child? Provide for her, love her,
teach her, protect her, be responsible for her well-being for
the next eighteen years or so... and beyond?

The prospect was overwhelming. But when she gazed
down at Daisy, she felt as if she could move mountains if
need be.

Jessie felt a great relief in simply admitting the truth to
herself. She shut off the light and slipped under the covers. She positioned herself at the edge of the bed, where
she could still see Daisy in the moonlight and keep a hand
on the basket.

But how would she do it? She didn't know. She didn't know the laws about these situations. Clint had mentioned couples on waiting lists, looking for babies. But she had to have some chance, didn't she? After all, she was the one who had found Daisy.

Something told her that she couldn't look to Clint for any help in this matter. In fact, she would probably do best if he didn't even know of her plans. She guessed that he would disapprove openly of the idea and maybe even try to block her efforts.

If only Aunt Claire was around to talk to, Jessie thought. But Aunt Claire was on her way to India by now. Jessie had the itinerary someplace, but she didn't want to trouble Claire on her holiday. No, she'd have to take this one on by herself.

The first place to start was probably with the social worker on the case, Alice Hoag. Clint had mentioned her name just this evening. Jessie wondered if it was the same Alice Hoag who had gone to her high school. Alice had been her lab partner in chemistry class. And they'd been on the girls' basketball team together. Alice had a wicked slam dunk.

She'd call the hospital herself tomorrow morning, first thing. Maybe Alice would help her out and tell her how she could keep Daisy. If Alice wouldn't help her, she'd find someone else who would.

"If it's possible any way in this world, baby girl," Jessie whispered to Daisy, "I'm going to do it."

Clint thought it best not give Jessie any warning. As he drove toward her house the next day at about noon, he tried not think of how much she was going to hate him. Last night on the phone she'd asked him if he thought she could come along for the ride to Whitewood when he took

Daisy. Hearing her sweet voice, the way she sounded when she talked about the baby, he'd almost caved in.

But somehow he'd managed to say no. Why drag out the agony? Taking that baby from her was going to be hell. Easily the hardest assignment he'd had to face in a long, long time. He wondered again, for the thousandth time perhaps, why he'd ever agreed to let her care for the child in the first place.

Damn it, but he did the strangest things around that woman. He didn't know what it was about her—New England witchery perhaps? Whatever it was, he had to keep his guard up. Double it, in fact. He couldn't trust himself. And he couldn't afford any more slipups.

Clint knocked hard on Jessie's front door. He braced himself. As soon as she'd see him, she'd guess why he'd come.

Jessie swung open the door. She looked surprised at first to see him, as he'd expected. Then her face lit up with her wonderful smile. At the sight of her, he felt that little telltale "ping" in his chest, like an engine with a busted piston. He tried his best to ignore it.

"Come on in, Clint," she greeted him. "Daisy is down for a nap and I just put on some coffee. Would you like a cup?"

Daisy was napping. He hadn't even thought of that glitch. How could he grab the baby and run if she was down for a nap?

"I—well, sure. I'll take a cup of coffee." He followed Jessie into the kitchen and sat at the big oak table. He took off his hat and placed it on an empty chair.

Clint tried not to follow her around the room with his eyes, but he couldn't help it. Every since he'd left her here, two days ago, he'd been watching her in his mind's eye— as he drove around the county on empty, snow-covered roads; as he lay in his lonely bed, trying not to think about her. Not to think about the next time he might be with her.

So go see her again, he told himself. It'll bring you down to earth. She's just a woman—an attractive woman, yes. But just a woman, after all, like all the rest.

Now, here she was, in all her glory. Not like all the rest at all. More wonderful in fact than he had remembered. And close enough to reach out and touch, if he dared.

She had on a big gold-colored turtleneck woven out of some type of soft, fuzzy-looking wool and a pair of worn-out, rather tight jeans. He usually didn't like the way women looked in jeans that were too tight, but with her slim hips and long legs, Jessie was certainly the exception to the rule. As she bent to reach something on a low shelf in the refrigerator, he noted how the worn denim hugged her sweet bottom to perfection. And felt a telltale tightening at a very critical point in the fabric of his own jeans.

Then she straightened up and walked across the room to get the coffee cups. He loved watching her move and that would have to be enough; just like this, watching her move about on those long, show-girl legs, so gracefully, so purposefully, her long reddish gold hair floating out behind her.

The mere sight of her was almost enough to make him forget why he had come in the first place.

Almost. But not quite.

Finally she sat down at the table across from him and poured the coffee. "God, it seems like such luxury just to sit down for a minute and drink some coffee." She laughed. "Daisy has really kept me running. Not that I minded a second of it, though," she assured him. "She is such a sweet baby. You know, after that first night, she's hardly cried at all."

Clint couldn't bear to look her in the eye. He picked up the creamer and poured way too much milk into his coffee.

"Jessie, you know why I came, don't you?" he asked her quietly. "I have to take Daisy over to Whitewood today."

"Yes, I know that." Jessie nodded.

He drew in a breath, expecting the worst. She'd argue with him about her. She'd try to delay it. She'd probably even cry. Yes, she'd definitely cry, he thought. What then? He'd want to put his arms around her, but he didn't dare allow himself to touch her again. Hell, if he touched her, he'd kiss her. And if he kissed her, he'd want to... Well, they'd probably wind up in bed before this cup of coffee cooled off.

"I have something I want to tell you," she said. Her quiet tone of voice hinted at some greater enthusiasm. "Some very good news—"

Clint stared at her with a puzzled expression. What was going on here? Why wasn't she hysterical? What news?

The doorbell sounded and Jessie rose to answer it.

"Just wait here a second. I'll be right back," she assured him.

"Jessie?" he called after her as she dashed out of the kitchen. "What's going on?"

He sat back in his chair and sipped his coffee. He heard the sound of another woman's voice in the foyer, a very gleeful female greeting. It sounded as if Jessie were greeting some long-lost friend.

Wasn't it like her? he reminded himself. He'd only know the woman for a little over two days, but he already knew the way she operated. Just when you thought you had it all figured out, she waved her little hand and changed the whole ball game.

Jessie appeared at the doorway to the kitchen again, followed by a woman about her age with shiny, chin-length dark hair and bright brown eyes. Jessie's visitor was dressed for business, in a stylish dark green wool suit, and she carried a worn leather briefcase that bulged with manila file folders.

"Clint, I'd like you to meet Alice Hoag," Jessie said smoothly. "I know you two have spoken over the phone a few times about Daisy, but I don't think you've ever actually met, have you?" she asked Alice.

"Hello, Clint," Alice said warmly as she stretched out her hand to him. "You've taken such an interest in Daisy's case. I was really looking forward to meeting you and thanking you personally."

Clint shook Alice's hand, uncharacteristically at a loss for words. "Nice to meet you, too" was the best he could manage.

He shot a quick glance at Jessie, who had taken off in search of another coffee cup for Alice. She was snickering into her big fuzzy turtleneck; he knew it. If not snickering, then at least having a quiet private laugh at catching him so off guard. But what in heaven's name did all this mean?

"I had to visit with a client in town this morning, so it was no trouble at all for me to stop by here to do Jessie's interview and home visit before I head back to the hospital," Alice explained as she sat down.

"Interview and home visit?" Clint didn't know all that much about how social workers operated in a case like this, but it sounded as if Jessie were applying to be a foster parent. He leaned back in his chair and folded his arms across his chest. "I thought you were here to take the baby to the hospital," he said to Alice.

"Uh, no, not at all," she said hesitantly. Now it was Alice's turn to look puzzled. She also glanced quickly at Jessie, who had just joined them at the table. "Jessie and I spoke this morning about Daisy. And her feelings about the baby going into the system—" She paused. "Didn't she tell you any of this?"

"Alice is going to help me get custody of Daisy," Jessie cut in. "I'm applying to be her temporary guardian until the investigation is over and she can be adopted."

"At which point you'll hand her over to her adopting parents?" he asked.

Jessie looked him straight in the eye. "I want to adopt her."

Clint exhaled a big breath. "Adopt her? You don't know what you're talking about," he burst out. "I know you have strong feelings for the child," he added in a softer voice. "Who wouldn't under the circumstances? And, well...you're the type to fall in love with a baby. But the truth of the matter is that just because you found her, you don't have any special legal rights in the matter. She's not a little stray puppy that you're bringing home from the pound, you know," he argued.

He turned to Alice Hoag for support in his argument. She answered him with a disapproving stare.

"It's true that Jessie's finding the baby doesn't give her any special claim. But what exactly is your objection to Jessie going through the process and being named as the temporary guardian—or even adopting this baby, Sheriff?"

He willed himself not to look at Jessie as he spoke, yet he could see her, out of the corner of his eye, sitting up straight and tense, her fingers twisting together on the tabletop.

"I think a kid deserves two parents, first off. It might not be the fashionable position, but that's what I think. There are too many kids living with one or the other because of divorce, as it is. Why add to the problem by letting single women—or men, for that matter—adopt a child like this one?" he stated bluntly.

Jessie sat with her head bowed, staring down into her coffee. She didn't even look up at him when he finished.

"Is that your only objection?" Alice asked evenly. "There's nothing personal that you'd care to go on record with? Nothing that would undermine Jessie's fitness in the eyes of the court as a suitable guardian?"

Why, the woman didn't know the first thing about taking care of a baby until I showed her, he wanted to say.

But then he looked over at Jessie. She was staring at him now, her brown eyes wide and shining. Like a deer, trapped in the headlights of an oncoming truck.

He sighed. Well, he was going to swerve hard to the right just in time. Carrying out his official duty and collecting the baby was one thing. But he wasn't going to be the one to burst this adoption-plan bubble. He'd leave that unsavory job to some crusty old judge who hadn't even heard the news that women had gotten the vote. She wouldn't get far with this application. Not around here anyway. Hope Springs wasn't exactly New York or Los Angeles.

"No, nothing," Clint said finally. He heard Jessie exhale an audible sigh.

"You're sure?" Alice prodded. "You were the officer who made out the report when the baby was found. If there's anything at all you'd care to add, Clint, now is the time. In fact, your appraisal of Jessie's caretaking these past few days is going to be an important part of her application."

"Clint, I've already told Alice how you helped me," Jessie told him. "I mean, how I didn't know much about taking care of Daisy and how you brought all that stuff over and gave that me that crash baby-care course."

"Yes, Jessie told me all about that. That was very good of you," Alice said approvingly.

"Anybody else would have done the same," Clint said, brushing off the compliment. "It didn't take much. Jessie seemed to know what to do naturally."

"So you would say she did a good job taking care of Daisy?" Alice asked. She had pulled out a folder from her briefcase and was now writing something on a big yellow pad.

"Look, if you need some kind of official statement, you can contact me at my office," Clint answered tensely. He still wouldn't let himself look at Jessie, though he could feel her looking at him. "I believe that's the way these things are supposed to go, aren't they?" he challenged Alice.

Alice did not appear the least bit flustered by Clint's animosity. "I can interview you at your office, or take your statement by phone if you prefer," she said smoothly.

"Yes, that's what I'd prefer," he replied. His face was a stony mask as he reached over the empty chair and retrieved his hat. "If I'm no longer needed here, I'd better be going," he said, rising from his chair.

"I'll walk you to the door," Jessie offered.

"That's all right." He lightly touched her shoulder as he passed behind her, willing her to remain seated. "I can find my way out."

"I'll get in touch with you tomorrow, Clint. I'd like to complete this report quickly," Alice said. "But I think what we have so far is a good start."

"Here's the number at the station house and at home,'' he said, handing Alice his card. "Goodbye, ladies. And good luck," he said pointedly, staring straight at Jessie.

She watched him go, biting down on her lower lip. He seemed mad at her, but she guessed it was understandable. She'd sort of bushwhacked him with Alice, if the truth be told. But turnabout was only fair play. Hadn't he tried to sneak up on her to take Daisy away?

She'd been right about his objections to single motherhood. And Jessie wondered if he planned to toss a monkey wrench into the whole thing. Well, she'd just have to wait and see. It seemed that once again her fate was in Clint Bradshaw's hands.

As she turned her attention back to Alice, she realized that as of this point, Clint's job with Daisy was over. He had no further official reason to call here, or stop by. For all Jessie knew, except for chance encounters that came about in a small town, she might not hear from him, or see him for a long time. The realization made her sad, for the truth was, he'd barely left her house five minutes ago and she already missed him terribly.

Right after Alice reviewed the applications and finished her interview, Jessie packed up Daisy and headed into town. She knew she'd been away from the café for only two days, but it felt like longer.

Jessie had not been in the café since Christmas Eve, but Sophie, Ivy and Charlie had gone back to work the day after Christmas. Her experienced, sometimes cantankerous crew had taken her instructions over the phone and had somehow managed to run the place without her for an entire day and a half.

With Daisy in her arms, she trudged up the snowy sidewalk and flung open the door. The usual lunch crowd filled the dining area and counter. While Ivy worked the

tables, Sophie served the counter customers and worked
the register. Through the narrow pass-through window
behind the counter, Charlie's apron-clad figure could be
seen racing around the kitchen.

Normally, Jessie's entrance would barely be noticed at
such a hectic time of day. But today, as she came through
the door, all conversation stopped. All eyes turned toward her and the baby in her arms.

Daisy, wearing a pink Polarfleece suit that Clint had
bought her, and a pink wool hat with little yellow ears
sewed on top, was a vision of cuteness. She turned her face
toward the crowd and gazed around.

"The baby's here!" Sophie announced in her boister-
ous, booming voice. "Jessie finally got here with the
baby!"

"Would you look at that baby!" Gus Parker shouted.
Gus was a tough old man who ran a junkyard and scrap-
metal lot just outside of town. He rarely spared a smile,
no less a greeting, even for folks he'd known his whole
life. But, shocking Jessie, Gus hopped off his stool and
came closer to greet the baby. "What a living doll. Hello,
sweetheart," he cooed in a baby voice.

"What a honey!" Betty Dudley, who owned the dress
shop down the street, came up and tickled Daisy under the
chin.

"Look at her hair," Ida Lewis, who owned the phar-
macy on Main Street, commented to Betty. "Look at
those curls—"

At Betty's bidding, Jessie removed Daisy's little hat.
"Oh, my heavens!" Betty gasped. "Isn't she an angel!"

"What an angel!" Homer Jones, who worked in the
Crafty Yankee Gift Shop echoed. "Jessie, she's absolutely precious."

Within two minutes of her stepping over the threshold, every café patron and employee had gathered around Jessie and Daisy, as if greeting a world famous celebrity.

"Okay now, give the little baby some room," Sophie insisted, using her ample figure to clear a path up to the counter for Jessie and Daisy. "You'll all get your turn to meet her. One by one. We don't want to scare the little thing now."

Still cooing and oozing adulation, Daisy's admirers backed off a bit and allowed Jessie to bring her to a quiet area near the register. Ivy ran out to Jessie's Jeep and retrieved the car seat, which Jessie set up on a table for Daisy to sit in.

"People have been stopping by all day, asking about the baby," Sophie told Jessie. "They've been leaving off presents for her, too."

"Presents?" Jessie asked. She wasn't all that surprised that Daisy was big news in the small town. Naturally, people would be eager to get a look at an abandoned baby—one who was left on Christmas Eve, no less. But presents?

"I'll say," Sophie repeated. "Looks like Santa dumped an entire sleighload for this little sprout. There's clothes and blankets and baby quilts. A bunch of teddy bears—I sort of lost count of the stuffed animals. A rocking horse and a high chair and a portable crib. Brand-new in the box, too," she added.

"A portable crib?" Jessie couldn't quite believe it. She picked up Daisy and headed for the storeroom. As Sophie had described, it was so packed with cartons and gift-wrapped boxes, she could barely fit through the door.

"Where did all this stuff come from?" she asked.

"From folks," Charlie explained in his typically bland manner. "Everyone heard about you finding the baby and figured it needed stuff. Oh, isn't she a little sweet potato?" he added, smiling down at Daisy. "Heh, Daisy— look at Uncle Charlie," he said, making a silly face that showed his two gold teeth to advantage.

"Stop that now, you old buzzard. You'll scare her," Sophie scolded.

Daisy's big brown eyes widened. Then she gurgled and laughed. Charlie laughed and slapped his thigh. "I told you I was good with babies, old woman," he said to Sophie. "You just didn't believe me."

"Oh, shush up, I'm talking to Jessie," Sophie said curtly. Then turning back to her boss she said, "We heard you're going to keep her."

"Who told you that?" Jessie asked.

"Folks been saying it all day," Charlie answered.

"Folks, huh?" Jessie asked. Charlie nodded. News sure traveled fast in this town. Jessie had lived here all her life but the speed at which gossip traveled still astounded her.

"Is it true?" Ivy asked eagerly, peeking over Sophie's shoulder. "I could do some baby-sitting for you sometime, Jessie. When I'm not working here. Or, at school, I mean."

"I could sit for that little one, too," Sophie countered. "It'd be no trouble at all. The house is all babyproofed and fully equipped from the grandchildren, you know."

"You keep her, Jessie," Charlie advised. "You found her and all. Why, you'd be a fine mother for that little girl. I can see the way she's clinging to you. She loves you already."

"You really think so?" Jessie's heart warmed at Charlie's observation. She knew him to be unfailingly honest—even if he sometimes hurt people's feelings.

"Oh, she really knows you already," Sophie assured her. "Look how nice and calm she is sitting with you. Even with all these annoying people gawking at her."

"I do want to keep her," Jessie confided. She gazed down at Daisy, who was playing with a set of plastic measuring spoons that Ivy dangled in front her. "And I really do love her."

"Well, that settles it then, doesn't it?" Sophie said. "And don't be afraid about going this alone, Jessie. We're all here to help you. Just like family. Isn't that right?" she asked the others.

Ivy and Charlie heartily agreed. As Jessie gazed around at her friends—and the truckload of presents in the storeroom—she felt so very fortunate. She'd never realized how a baby could bring out the soft side of people, the generous and kind spirit that you usually saw only around the holidays. Now, if only the bureaucratic side of things worked in with Daisy's adoption. But her kind-hearted friends couldn't help her there.

"I'm going to try to adopt her. But it won't be easy," Jessie told them. "I think I'd better not count on it working out," she said in a careful tone.

"Now you can't go into the fight of your life thinking like that," Sophie scolded her. "You've got to think positive. Stick to your guns. You've got the baby. Just let them try to take her away."

"It's not that simple, Sophie. It has to go to court. A judge has to decide," Jessie began to explain.

"I'll stand up in court for you, hon," Sophie promised. "Just let me talk to that judge. Why, I known you all your life. You're way too modest to let people know half of the nice things you do for folks around here. All the free meals to whoever walks in here with a sad story. All the food you send over to the school, and the charities. All the money you probably give them, too. No one in their right mind would refuse you after I go through with pleading your case."

"Thanks, Sophie." Jessie smiled at her. "If I need any character witnesses, I'll let you know."

Ivy, who had gone back to the dining room to wait on the customers, suddenly burst through the kitchen doors. "Hey, we'd better get back out there. People are screaming for their orders."

"Tell them I'm cooking as fast as I can," Charlie shouted at her. "If they want one of them rubber, hockey-puck burgers just shoved at you through a little window, they know where to go."

"Let me handle them, honey. I know what to say," Sophie said calmly to Ivy. She smoothed her apron over her big stomach and hips and headed out to the dining area. "People ought to understand today is sort of a holiday. For goodness' sake, it's not every day Jessie brings her new baby in here."

Sophie sailed through the kitchen doors and Ivy scurried after her, carrying out orders with two hands. Charlie got back to the stove and began some of his speed cooking. Jessie sat with Daisy in her lap, watching the action. She kissed the top of the baby's head, and Daisy's soft curls tickled her nose.

Up until now, no one but Alice and Clint had known for sure that she hoped to adopt Daisy. But telling Sophie, Ivy and Charlie had somehow made the whole dream feel as if it actually could come true. Jessie smiled. Yes, this could really work out for her. And wouldn't that be wonderful?

The week passed quickly as Jessie tried to get into some routine that combined caring for Daisy and running the café. With Charlie's help, she hauled home all the baby gifts, cleaned out the storeroom and began to convert it into an away-from-home nursery for Daisy. By storing baby supplies both at home and in the café, Jessie was able to meet Daisy's every need when she took the baby along to work with her.

When she wasn't taking care of Daisy or working, Jessie sat up nights, studying every book on baby care she could get her hands on. She'd cleaned off the shelf devoted to child care at the local bookstore and did just about the same at the library. If anybody of any merit had written anything worthwhile about babies, Jessie was determined to read it. Within a week's time, she knew the best method to clean out Daisy's ears and trim her tiny nails. She knew if Daisy was eating, sleeping and even dirtying her diapers as much as the typical four-month-old infant.

She offered Daisy toys designed to stimulate her senses and develop her eye-to-hand coordination. She was vigilantly on the prowl for cradle cap and diaper rash and well prepared for Daisy's potential episodes of teething, hiccups and inconsolable crying. And she practically couldn't wait to teach Daisy the classics of babyhood, like clap-hands and peek-a-boo.

Naturally, Sophie and other experienced mothers were always on hand to offer Jessie advice. Whether she asked for it or not. As far as Jessie could see, there were no pat answers to parenting. The experts in the field seemed to disagree on as many topics as they concurred upon. She could already see that you were largely left to your own devices, to rely upon your common sense, your ability not to panic and an unlimited store of patience.

During the week, Jessie heard from Alice several times. The first calls mainly had to do with details of Jessie's application and Alice's interest in how things were going with the baby. Finally, at the end of the week Alice called to tell Jessie that she'd been approved as Daisy's temporary guardian. Jessie let out an audible sigh of relief when Alice told her.

"Jessie, you sound as if you thought you wouldn't be approved," Alice said in surprise.

"Well, I was hoping it would work out. But I wasn't sure what was going to happen. I wasn't sure what Clint would say when you interviewed him privately," she added.

Alice had made a big point of how much the approval would depend on Clint's input. She knew he had it in his power to ruin everything for her. And considering his reaction to the news that she wanted to adopt Daisy, Jessie didn't think that was out of the range of possibilities.

"Sheriff Bradshaw was cooperative when I spoke with him privately. And a lot less . . . difficult," Alice told her. "The information he gave me is confidential, of course. But I can tell you that he had some very complimentary things to say about your ability to care for the baby. And your suitability as her guardian."

"He did?" Jessie said in surprise. "I thought he was going to tank me. You heard what he said at my house about single mothers."

"Well, I suspect the conversation pressed some personal buttons," Alice replied. "Oh, he got on his soapbox about all that again. But he didn't have a negative word to say about what he had observed between you and the baby."

"That's—interesting." Jessie didn't know what else to say.

Her first impulse was to call Clint and thank him for helping her out. Then she thought the better of it. He'd made it plain that he didn't want to get involved with her. Unfortunately, that realization hadn't helped her to think about him any less. Calling him would just make things worse. And she didn't think she could handle one of those monosyllabic, Mr. Impersonal conversations again.

To her surprise, Jessie had the chance to thank Clint personally, when he stopped by the café a few days later. It was a quiet time, around three in the afternoon. After the lunch rush and well before the dinner crowd.

Jessie was sitting at the counter, reading one of her baby books and underlining passages with a thick yellow marker. Though she heard the bells on the door ring, she didn't even look up when Clint entered.

"Studying for your final exams, Jessie?" he teased her. "Don't worry. I hear the teacher is marking on a curve."

She lifted her head. He was standing right next to her, looking down at her with a playful smile that lit up his dark blue eyes and caused those elusive dimples to deepen in his cheeks. The indescribably handsome sight of him took her breath away.

She forgot for a moment that he'd kissed her silly Christmas Day and then had the nerve to apologize for it. She forgot how he had warned her off in so many words and left her feeling so damned foolish. She reminded herself that she hardly knew this man. And a lot of what she knew about him, she didn't even like. She forgot everything...except how much she'd missed him. And how good it made her feel, to simply see him standing there, smiling at her. As if maybe he'd missed her a little, too.

"I'm just reading about... babies," she admitted. She put the book aside and turned around on the stool to face him.

"Now, why doesn't that surprise me?" He sat down on the stool next to her and turned his body to face her. "I heard from Alice that you're Daisy's temporary guardian."

"That's right." Jessie nodded. She looked down at the book again and then back up at him. "I wanted to thank you. Alice said that your interview helped."

"I didn't say anything special." He shrugged a big shoulder. "Just answered her questions." He paused and looked at her. "I have some news for you, too."

"Oh? About Daisy, you mean?" Jessie asked.

"The investigation is almost complete. It doesn't look like the police will ever find out who left her here."

"That's great!" Jessie could not contain her excitement. Without thinking, she jumped off the stool and straight into Clint's arms. "That's the best news in the world. Thank you so much for telling me, Clint—"

She suddenly realized that she was hugging him. Not just a quick, friendly type hug, but one of the long-lost-lover variety, with arms entwined around his neck and her head burrowed against his broad shoulder and warm, strong neck.

For better or worse, he didn't seem to mind. In fact, he was hugging her back in just the same way. She could feel his warm lips resting for a second on the top of her head and his arms wrapped around her waist, practically lifting her feet off the ground.

Then suddenly he returned to his senses. And so did Jessie. They quickly, but awkwardly, disengaged from their embrace.

"Well, don't get too excited. It's not official yet," he warned her. "Some new scrap of evidence could pop up even at this late date."

"But you're pretty sure it's over, aren't you?" she prodded.

"Yes, I think they'll close it tomorrow or the next day."

"Yes!" Jessie pumped her fist in the air over her head. "I'll have to call Alice right away. There's so much more paperwork we have to fill out for the adoption."

"You're still planning on going through with that?" Clint's expression darkened. "You haven't changed your mind, have you?"

Jessie felt a little fist tighten around her heart. Why did he have to be so disapproving? The one person in the world who she wanted on her side. Why did he have to take on the voice of the opposition?

"Why would I have changed my mind? If anything, having Daisy these past two weeks has made me even more determined to adopt her."

"I thought that seeing how difficult it is to run this business and handle a baby on your own might have made you see things a little more sensibly, Jessie."

Yes, it *was* hard to run the business and take care of Daisy. Some days, she didn't know whether she was coming or going. It was a supreme juggling act that Jessie hadn't even come close yet to mastering. But she wasn't about to admit all that to Clint.

And besides, the decision had very little to do with good sense. She didn't care if the café was running like a comedy show and she felt as if she'd been hit by a truck at the end of each day. When she looked into Daisy's little face, it made up for everything.

"I am getting along just fine. Everything is totally under control," she insisted. "Ask anybody."

Charlie came roaring out the kitchen and they both looked up at him.

"For Christmas' sake, Jessie, I am clean out of eggs again! What do you expect me to do tomorrow morning, sit down and cluck?"

"Calm down, Charlie," Jessie instructed, herding him back into the kitchen. "I'll take care of it right away. Why don't you check to see if we need anything else and make me a list?"

"I made you a list yesterday. Did you lose that one, too?" the irate cook grumbled as he headed back into the kitchen. "For pity's sake, this place is a loony bin lately...."

Jessie returned to Clint. He didn't say a word. Then again, he didn't have to.

"He gets like that all the time. Cooks have their moods, you know," she explained.

"Yeah, I've heard," Clint replied. He crossed his arms over his broad chest and stretched his long legs out in front of him.

He did have a glorious body, she noted in some distant part of her brain. She hated herself for being so distracted by his looks, but she couldn't help it. As he gazed at her soberly, she slipped behind the counter, and busied herself with drying some glasses.

"You must think I'm pretty awful, coming in here and telling you how to run your life," he said finally. "Don't you?"

"Awful?" Jessie focused her attention on the glass she was drying. "I don't think you're awful...exactly. Narrow-minded and sort of inflexible, maybe—" She glanced at him over her shoulder. "But I wouldn't call you awful."

"Thanks—" he winced "—for sparing my feelings."

She turned to face him squarely, with only the counter-top standing between them. "I do wonder about one thing, though. Why are you so dead set against me adopting Daisy? I mean, what's it to you?"

"Maybe I don't want to see you go through this whole process and be devastated when things don't work out and the court takes Daisy away," he said quietly. "Even with Alice in your corner, the cards are pretty much stacked against you."

"That's not the way I see it at all," she replied sharply. "And Alice says my chances are good. Even very good."

"What do you expect Alice to say?" he replied in an even tone. "She's your friend, isn't she?"

"And you're not quite a friend, so you'll tell me the cold, harsh truth. Is that it?" Jessie asked him bluntly, one hand on her hip.

"Maybe I'm more of a friend than anyone, Jessie," he said, his blue eyes darkening like storm clouds. "Maybe it's harder to tell someone something they don't want to hear. But you do it because you care about them."

He was actually admitting that he cared about her? Jessie allowed the thought to register only briefly. If she dwelled on it for too long, she'd be liable to melt at his feet into a puddle of pure, unadulterated mush.

"Okay, let's have it out here and now." She stood facing him and slapped one hand down on the countertop hard enough to rattle a nearby sugar bowl. "Why do you insist that the court won't grant this adoption? Why do you say I'm wasting my time?"

"Just look at your life as a judge on this case would," he said harshly. "You're self-employed, you work more than full-time running this café, and you don't have a husband. Frankly, I don't believe that you're thinking much about Daisy. A child deserves two parents. I think that the courts around here are fairly conservative and will agree with me on that point at least.

"And besides all that," he added, before she could get in a word, "I think you still have some soft, fuzzy fantasy about raising a child. It isn't one long, cuddly baby-lotion commercial. It's a hard, thankless job and it doesn't get any easier as they get older.''

Once again his deeply felt words gave Jessie good reason to wonder about his past. How did he know so much about raising kids, and why did he feel so deeply about her situation? But she knew that if she prodded him right now on that question, she'd get nowhere. And she was also too eager to counter his arguments against her adopting Daisy.

"Are you quite through?" she asked testily.

"Yes, I am." He nodded at her. "Not that a single word of what I've said has sunk in, I gather."

"Look, I was raised by my aunt, completely on her own, and I had a very happy, satisfying childhood. So don't tell me that a single parent can't raise a happy, well-adjusted child—"

"That's not what I meant exactly," he cut in.

"And about my being a working mother...." she interrupted. "More than half of the women today work outside the home in some fashion. Most of them don't even have the luxury of making their own hours as I can and of keeping their child with them all day if they want to," she added. "I've arranged to spend less time here by hiring a new waitress and having Ivy take over as manager on nights and weekends. And I've fixed up the storeroom into a nice little nursery for Daisy so that she's completely comfortable whenever I bring her here. She's back there napping right now. Snug as a bug.''

By the time Jessie had finished her tirade, she was standing nose to nose with Clint and was out of breath from arguing.

"Well, I guess that covers everything." He sat back, a smug look on his handsome face. "Except of course, your lack of a husband. Which is probably going to be the deal breaker."

"Look, if I need to find a man to marry me in order to adopt Daisy, then that's just what I'll do," she countered. Although she sure hoped it wouldn't come to that.

"You'll find a husband, just like that?" He snapped his fingers.

"It's not as if I've never had any offers," she replied defensively. "There are men...in my life." She turned her back on him and took up her dish towel again. It wasn't a total lie. She was asked on dates from time to time. And there was always Charlie. He counted, didn't he? "Marriage has just not been that great a priority for me. But I will do what I have to do to adopt Daisy. Count on it, Clint," she said firmly.

Men in her life? Who were these men, he wanted to know. She hadn't mentioned any men in her life when they'd talked about this relationship stuff on Christmas Day. But now there were plenty of men. And she was bound and determined to do what she had to do.

He gazed at her and swallowed hard. She was all fired up, with her big brown eyes shining, her cheeks flushed and her mussed hair flying loose in all directions from its haphazard upswept style. Yes, he was sure she'd had her offers, from marriage to no-strings affairs—and everything in between. He supposed she had her pick of the men—single and otherwise—who came through here.

"Well, Jessie, sounds to me like you've got it covered," he replied quietly. He slipped down off the stool, picked up his hat and yanked it down on his head. "Why don't you just marry the next man that strolls in here and live happily ever after?''

"Maybe I will," she replied tartly.

As if on cue, Charlie chose that moment to pop through the kitchen doors again. "I'm down to my last onion, Jessie. And I can't go rooting around the cellar, looking for the emergency supply," he complained. "My bum knee is paining me something awful."

"I'll go, Charlie. Just give me a minute," Jessie said, her eyes fixed on Clint. Clint glanced at Charlie and back to Jessie.

"Well, here's the lucky fellow, right now," Clint said in a gruff tone as he headed for the door. "I hope you'll be very happy together. See you around, Jessie."

"See you," she said tersely. She watched his tall broad-shouldered figure disappear through the door and then pass quickly by the café's front window.

Charlie cleared his throat, obviously trying to draw her attention. She turned to him. "Yes?"

"That poor fella's got it bad for you, boss," he said, laughing to himself. He scratched the back of his bald head, then smoothed down a few remaining wisps of gray hair. "Does he ever."

"What in the world are you talking about, Charlie?" she snapped. "Get back in the kitchen, will you please? We're not going to be ready for the dinner customers."

"Uh-huh. Whatever you say." Charlie nodded as he shuffled back toward the kitchen with a huge smirk on his face. "Hell, anybody can see it. Poor fella's got his tail tied in a knot," she heard him mutter. "Just letting him pine away. Howling at the moon. Turning himself inside out...."

"Silly old man," Jessie grumbled to herself. That would be the day when Clint Bradshaw was turning himself inside out over her.

Five

The moment he strode out of the café, Clint made a solemn vow—another solemn vow—to steer clear of Jessie in every possible way. He'd said what he'd come to say. What she did now was her own damn business.

He wouldn't call her or stop by the café. He wouldn't ask their mutual acquaintances, like Alice Hoag, for news of Jessie and Daisy. And hardest of all, he wouldn't let himself fall into a pleasant warm daze of thinking about her, of fantasizing about how it would be if he ever had the chance to take her in his arms again and touch her and kiss her and—

Clint slammed the brakes on his runaway libido and shook his head. See, that's exactly what I mean, he coached himself. Think about something else. Think about the reports you have to write up tonight. Think about that cute ambulance driver from Woodstock who asked you for your phone number. What was her name

again? Suzy? Sally? Sandy? Hell, think about those basketball tickets for next Sunday night....

It amazed him, when he considered how Jessie had
crossed his path only a few weeks ago, yet had somehow
succeeded in totally messing up his mind. After all the
women in all the towns he traveled through in the past few
years, why did he have to feel this damned male-female
chemistry with her? What was it about the confounded
female that touched him so? That reached right in on a
direct line to his heart and gave it a jump start every time
she so much as looked at him?

It amazed him how she acted so strong and self-
sufficient all the time—as if she didn't need a friend in the
world—when to him, she often seemed just the opposite.
So damn trusting and vulnerable, so in need of someone
to help her, to hold her, to just wrap their arms around her
and protect her.

But one way or another, the woman needed a man
willing to make promises. Commitments. A permanent
arrangement. And therefore she could just mark him off
her dance card right now. That was what it all boiled
down to, didn't it?

He wanted her in the worst way. But he didn't want any
part of a permanent attachment. He just couldn't do it.
Not even for Jessie. And that was why he had to do his
damnedest to stay away from her and her café and her
abandoned baby and all her naive, heart-wrenching
dreams.

"I'm sorry, Jessie. But I have to tell you the truth, and
Judge Hall's record on adoption cases is no secret," Alice said. "Your application is very strong in every re-
spect. Except for the fact that you're unmarried."

"I understand," Jessie replied quietly. She and Alice sat in the living room. Jessie sat on the rocker feeding Daisy a bottle and Alice sat across from her, on the sofa. "I guess this isn't going to work out after all."

"Well, not necessarily—" Alice replied with a shrug. "You still have some time left before the case comes up. A few weeks maybe. A lot can happen in that time." Alice lifted her dark eyes for a moment and caught Jessie's gaze.

"Like me walking down the aisle, Alice? Is that what you mean?" Jessie laughed.

"You know I can't advise you to get married just to strengthen your position in court, Jessie," Alice replied, gathering up the papers that she'd spread out on the couch. "But just between you and me," she added, glancing up at Jessie briefly, "can't you find a friend who wouldn't mind...well, helping you out for a few months? Just until the adoption is finalized? It's not the most ethical suggestion, I know. But I also know how much you love Daisy," she added, glancing at the baby in Jessie's arms, "and what a wonderful mother you'd be...what a wonderful mother you already are to her."

Jessie felt her eyes get all watery. She wasn't sure if it was because of Alice's compliment, or due to the very real prospect of losing Daisy. Clint had been right after all, she reflected. She wondered if he would gloat when he heard that she was fighting a losing battle to keep Daisy.

"Thanks, Alice. You've been a real pal," she replied quietly.

She set Daisy's bottle down and lifted her up to a sitting position. Daisy smiled and waved her arms. She tilted her head backward to give Jessie an adorable upside-down look and Jessie dropped a quick kiss on the top of Daisy's head. "I need to give this problem some serious thought," she said to Alice.

By the next morning, Jessie had faced the harsh truth that she needed a husband, or would risk losing Daisy forever. But despite her bravado when Clint posed the question, how in heaven's name was she going to find a man to marry her in a few weeks?

Her best recourse, she decided, was to reply to some personal ads. Did loads of people meet that way? Jessie wasn't sure, but until she thought of something better, she'd have to give it a try.

When Sophie came to work at half past six the next morning, she found Jessie in the nearly empty café sitting at the counter with Daisy in her lap and circling likely prospects in the "Up Close and Personal" column in the local newspaper.

"'Lean, but not mean,'" Jessie read aloud to Daisy. "'Busy executive longing to share jazz, Jacuzzis and Japanese food. Michelle Pfeiffer look-alikes preferred.'"

Daisy gurgled and swatted the newspaper.

"Right—not for us," Jessie said to her. "Let's see, how about this one.... 'Iron Man, looking for his Heavy Metal Lady—Let's go dirt biking, bodybuilding and much more. Tattoos a plus.'" Jessie stared down at the baby. "No tattoos. I guess that leaves me out."

"Looking for a nice date, Jessie?" Sophie asked approvingly. She peered over Jessie's shoulder as she tied on her apron. "It's about time you did something to perk up your social life. There's plenty of men wouldn't mind dating a woman with a baby, you know."

"How about marrying a woman with a baby?" Jessie replied. "I'm not looking for a social life, Sophie. I need a husband."

"A husband? Did I hear you right?" Sophie stared at her and blinked.

Jessie nodded. "Alice says that since I'm not married, I don't have a very good chance of winning custody of Daisy. I know it sounds crazy, but I need to find a husband. Fast."

"Well, what were you planning on doing?" Sophie asked. "Proposing to some stranger on the first date? I don't think that will get you very far. Men are skittish, you know. They scare easy," she warned her.

"Not on the *first* date, Sophie—" Jessie replied. Daisy grabbed a teaspoon off the counter and waved it around happily. Jessie shifted her to her other knee so she couldn't grab anything else. "I thought I'd go out with a few prospects this week, sort of check them out," she explained. "Then I'd pick the best of the lot and explain my problem. I thought maybe if I found some guy who wanted to get married anyway, he might be talked into helping me out and giving a temporary situation a try. With maybe a dowry thrown in," she added quietly.

"A dowry?" Sophie boomed. "You mean money? You mean you're going to find a man in the newspaper and pay him to marry you? Well, now I've heard everything—"

"Sophie—not so loud!" Jessie admonished. "Everyone in the place is going to hear you."

"Oh, what's the difference?" Sophie waved off Jessie's complaint. She stepped behind the counter and started making a fresh pot of coffee. "Everyone is going to find out about it anyhow. Even if the usual gossip grapevine suddenly went out of operation, everyone in town wants to know every little thing about that baby and what you're doing to keep her and what's going to happen next."

As much as Jessie wanted to believe otherwise, she knew that what Sophie said was true. If she went through with this husband-hunt plan—and she knew she had to—everyone in town would know about it.

She sighed and stared back down at the paper without seeing a word. It was a bit humiliating, too, considering that everyone knew how Sam Kincaid had left her at the altar. Now, five years later, she was so desperate, she was going to bribe a man to marry her. Even if they knew that her purpose was to keep Daisy, everyone would be talking about it. Laughing in secret at her, she supposed. Oh, let them laugh, she said to herself.

But she wasn't really thinking about everyone. She was thinking only about Clint.

Daisy stirred in her lap. She grabbed at the corner of the newspaper and tore off a chunk of the page. "Oh, see one you liked, honey?" Jessie asked, laughing as she pried open Daisy's little hand. She read the scrap of paper out loud.

"'Computer Nut—User-friendly. Great hard drive. Looking for compatible software....'" Jessie paused and looked up at Sophie. "I think this is going to be more difficult than I thought."

The older woman shook her head in dismay as she walked off to take an order. "You got your work cut out for you, honey. Good luck."

Several days and several discouraging dates later, Jessie was almost ready to abandon her plan. Almost, but not quite. She stared down at Daisy while the baby consumed a bottle. She had to keep going, for Daisy's sake. Her date for the night had canceled, but Jessie knew it was only a temporary reprieve.

It was almost eleven o'clock. Daisy had gone to sleep at eight, but had a habit of waking at this time for one last bottle—her "nightcap," Jessie called it.

Having the night off from husband hunting had been a relief. Jessie wasn't sure she could take much more.

Was she asking so much? There had to be a man out there, Jessie reasoned, who was reasonably intelligent, sane, kindhearted and held down a steady job. Somebody who didn't wear a toupee, complain about his exwife or his allergies the whole night, or confide that as a child, he'd been abducted by aliens.

Was she asking too much? He didn't have to be perfect. It was only going to be a temporary situation. Yet they were going to be married and obliged to put up a convincing show for the outside world. At least for the court. Whenever Jessie tried to visualize the type of man who would fit the bill, Clint's unbidden image would pop into her head. She didn't know why that should be, when he'd made it perfectly clear that he was the last man on earth who'd agree to her offer. The very last.

Daisy finished her bottle and Jessie put her to bed. Jessie had fixed up a spare bedroom right next to her own as a nursery, decorated with a bright border of teddy bear wallpaper and a polished pine crib and chest. The shelves were filled with toys and books and other treasures Daisy had received as gifts.

Dressed in her robe and nightgown, Jessie wandered around the house, locking doors and turning off lights. She had just gotten under the covers and was about turn out her bedside lamp, when she heard someone knocking on the front door.

She couldn't imagine who could be stopping by at this hour. She slipped on her robe and peered out a bedroom window. She could see the front of the house, but she couldn't see who was at the door. Then she glanced at the driveway and spotted the county sheriff's car parked there, unmistakable, even in the darkness.

She went downstairs to the front door. "Who is it?" she asked, just to double-check.

"It's me. Clint," he answered gruffly. She pulled open the door and clutched the top of her robe together when she felt the cold air remind her that she wasn't exactly dressed for entertaining.

"May I come in?" he asked politely.

She wasn't aware until then that she had been staring at him. Staring at him as if he'd just landed on her doorstep from outer space.

"Uh, sure... come on in," she replied.

He started to move toward the door and then stopped. "You're alone? I mean, I'm not interrupting anything?"

"Of course I'm alone... except for Daisy." She gave him a puzzled expression and stepped aside, opening the door a bit wider.

"I didn't mean Daisy," he said quietly. He didn't smile at her, she noticed. His dark brows were drawn together in what might have been a scowl, or a look of deep concern. As he stepped through the door, he pulled off his hat and swept his hand through his thick dark hair.

Jessica drew in a sharp breath. And it had nothing to do with the cold air coming in from outdoors. He looked very handsome. As damn handsome as ever. Even with a day's shadow of beard on his lean cheeks and the little lines around eyes and mouth drawn a bit deeper.

He shrugged off his jacket and hung it and his hat on a coat tree in the foyer. "I hope I didn't wake you up. I wasn't really looking at the time," he explained, turning toward her. "I saw the light on upstairs."

"It's okay. I wasn't asleep." She shrugged and crossed her arms over her chest.

When he'd walked out of the café after their argument last week, Jessie could have sworn she wasn't going to hear from him for some time. The last thing she ever expected was to find him on her doorstep on a dark, cold night like this one.

"I need to talk to you," he said in a serious tone. "Can we go inside?"

"Sure—" She followed him into the living room. She sat down on one end of the couch but Clint remained standing. He looked down at her.

"I heard you're looking for a husband. Is it true?" he asked her point-blank.

"Oh, when did you hear that?" Jessie ran her tongue over her lips. This wasn't going to be easy. She knew he'd hear about it sooner or later, but to confront her face-to-face like this.... She was absolutely mortified.

"Marilee was gossiping over the radio," he said, mentioning the radio dispatch operator who worked at the station house.

"Must be a slow night if all Marilee's got to send over the airwaves is gossip about my love life," Jessie commented. She looked up at Clint, who paced back and forth across the room like a big, nervous cat. "So, did you race right over here to gloat? Or were you already in the neighborhood when you got the bulletin? I hope you didn't have to drive much out of your way."

The true, unvarnished answer to her question was that he had nearly driven his patrol car right off a mountainside when he first heard the news. Then he had pulled a hairpin U-turn across four lanes of traffic worthy of any Hollywood stunt driver, and driven straight to her house at about eighty miles per hour. Clint didn't bother to explain all that to her, however.

He stopped pacing and stood directly in front of her. He had come closer, too, so that she had to bend her head back to look into his eyes.

"You didn't answer my question," he replied almost harshly. "Are you looking for a husband, or not?"

"Yes, I am," she answered defensively. "Looks like I need to be married in order to adopt Daisy. Even in this modern age. But it should hardly come as a surprise to you, Clint. It seems that both you and the honorable Judge Hall share the same antiquated—dare I say, Neanderthal?—ideas about raising children."

Though she expected him to take offense at her last jab, he appeared to ignore it.

"Any prospects?" he asked bluntly.

"Uh, no. Not yet," she answered truthfully. "But I have a few more dates lined up this week. Something— rather someone—" she corrected herself "—acceptable is bound to turn up sooner or later."

"I can't believe you're doing this." He stared at her, then paced toward the fireplace. With his back toward her, he rested his hands on the mantel a moment, as if struggling to get his emotions under control.

Jessie rose and took a few steps toward him. She wasn't going to let him make her feel self-conscious or foolish or too scared to go through with her plan. Which, it suddenly seemed, had been his purpose in coming here. The realization made her angry.

"I've told you before, Clint. I'm willing to do what I have to do to keep Daisy. I meant what I said."

"I know you meant it, Jessie. That's what scares me," he said, turning around to face her. "But you can't just

grab some guy you find in the personal ads, and bam—
instant husband."

"Why not?" she countered, her hands on her hips.

"It's not safe. It's not responsible. It's definitely not
sane," he added. "That's three reasons...do I need to go
on?"

"Don't you think I've thought of all that?" she practically shouted at him. "And what gives you the right to
barge in here, and try to tell me what to do? This is hard
for me. Very hard. I know that everyone in town is getting a good laugh at this, besides."

"I'm not laughing at you," he said quite seriously. "I
don't think there's anything the least bit funny about it."

"Well, you're the only one in town then," she informed him. "But maybe that's because you don't know
the whole story," she added in a quieter voice. She looked
down at her robe and fiddled with the sash.

"The whole story?" His puzzled expression was unac-
countably attractive—and quite distracting to Jessie.
"What do you mean, the whole story? You haven't pulled
this stunt before, have you?"

"Oh, no. It's nothing like that—" She sighed and sat
down, wondering if she should tell him about her failed
engagement. It wasn't a story that showed her in the most
flattering light, but if he asked around, he was bound to
hear it from anybody in town. "It's just something that
happened to me a long time ago. And it makes this present situation seem rather...ironic," she began to explain, trying to adopt an detached, breezy tone. "And
even more embarrassing for me than it would be anyway."

She sighed. Then, with her mouth set in a resigned expression, she added, "But I want to adopt Daisy. And I'll
do anything to win her."

He sat down on the couch next to her. Not all that close, but not that far away, either. "Go on. I'm listening," he encouraged her.

"Well—" She stared straight ahead and clasped her hands together. "It was about five years ago. I was engaged to marry a man I'd known since childhood. His name is Sam Kincaid. His father has a real-estate office in town, right down the street from the café."

"Yes, I know who you mean," Clint said impatiently. "So you and Sam were engaged to be married. Then what?"

"Well, the wedding was set for Christmas Day. Just about the entire town showed up at the church. Except for the groom." She glanced at Clint, managing a small smile. "He sent a note, explaining how he had second thoughts about the whole thing and had left for Boston very early that morning." Jessie brushed a wayward curl behind her ear. "Uh, with a young lady who had been working as a secretary in his dad's office," she added, giving him the last dirty detail.

And though Jessie had managed to put on a brave front, she had to assume from the look in Clint's eyes that some of her battle scars still showed.

"You must have been hurt. Hurt bad," Clint said feelingly.

"Oh, I was," she admitted. "But I got over it and I know now that it was all for the best. I mean, I don't think Sam and I would have been very happy. It was sort of a puppy-love thing. He was right to end it—though he probably could have done it in a less spectacular way," she added with a little laugh.

"So you were the talk of the town, I guess," Clint observed.

"Oh, it was quite a story. Sometimes I think they're still talking about it," Jessie joked.

"It always seemed funny to me, how much people— even nice people—like to talk about someone else's pain."

"I've thought of that sometimes myself," Jessie said. "I've decided that it helps them to deal with their own."

"That's an interesting theory." Clint nodded. But even after all that, you'll do anything to keep Daisy, he reflected. Even if it means the entire town is gossiping about your private life, past and present.

"You must love her very much," he said.

"I do." Jessie looked up into his dark blue eyes and felt as if she were in danger of losing herself there, in the swirling blue waters that engulfed her senses like windswept ocean waves.

Neither of them spoke for what seemed like a very long time to Jessie. Then Clint said, "That guy you were engaged to marry, that Sam...he was a damn fool," he said thoughtfully.

"Thanks—" Jessie stared down at her lap again and pulled the edge of her robe over her bare knees. "But it was a long time ago. You don't have to say anything to make me feel better, Clint."

"I'm not saying it to make you feel better," he argued back at her. "I'm stating a plain fact...." His voice trailed off.

Didn't the woman own a damned mirror? Didn't she understand how sweet and sexy and just plain terrific she was? He wanted to tell her all that—and more.

But he couldn't say the words. He could only stare at her in the thoughtful, brooding way that Jessie now found familiar—though no less unsettling. And the way he was looking at her suddenly made her very conscious of how little she was wearing—and how sheer and clingy that limited amount of fabric was.

Jessie shifted, trying to unobtrusively pull the edge of her robe closed, which now gaped open across her chest, showing off the lace edge of her peach satin nightgown and an ample view of her bare breasts.

"If I wanted to make you feel better, I wouldn't say a word," Clint added in a quieter voice. "I'd just lean over—" Still staring into her eyes, he leaned toward her until his mouth was barely a breath away from her own. "And I'd do this."

He touched his lips to hers, softly at first, yet not in a way that was in any way questioning or hesitant, but as if he were savoring every moment of that first electric contact, as if he were savoring the very taste of her, like a rare, exotic delicacy he'd badly craved and had gone too long without.

As if confirming those wild, romantic impressions, Jessie heard him breathe out a long, deep sigh of pleasure. "Mmm, you taste so good," he murmured.

He lifted his hands to her hair and moved close to her on the couch. Jessie's arms wound around his big body instantly, her breasts pressed against his solid, muscular chest.

His questing mouth moved over hers with increasing pressure. The more he demanded, the more Jessie gave, answering and anticipating his every move. Her lips parted and her tongue entwined with his, engaging in a silent foray that was sometimes a duel, an enjoyable duel, a contest for control that heightened the senses and whet the appetite. And sometimes a sultry dance that presaged the ultimate joining and surrender.

Jessie felt herself sink back against the pillows, winding her arms around Clint as he stretched his long, lean body over hers. He took a moment to unhook the belt holster that held his gun and set it down on the floor. Then he settled himself on top of her again with a deep, soulful kiss. It felt so good—so wonderfully right—to hold him close, to feel his long muscular legs entwined with hers, his lips hungrily seeking and capturing her own.

His hands roamed over her body restlessly, dipping into the curve of her waist, gliding down her thigh, molding the curve of her bottom and urging her hips into his gathering heat. Her legs parted and she cradled his hips in the juncture of her thighs, and through the layers of denim and satin she could feel his hardened manhood, intimately pressed against her, throbbing with desire.

She wriggled beneath him and moaned with frustration at the layers of clothing that stood between them and complete satisfaction. "Clint, please—" she whispered against his mouth, her mind too muzzy to formulate a coherent sentence.

"Please what, Jessie?" He chuckled deeply. "Please stop?" He lifted himself up over her, leaning his weight on his elbows and shifting his hips ever so slightly so that their contact became even more a pantomime of a complete union—and raising Jessie's level of passionate frustration even a few notches higher. "Or please continue?"

As he had calculated, he was instantly rewarded with Jessie's low moan as she matched his movements and fitted herself even closer to his hot, throbbing body.

"Please don't stop," she whispered seductively, feeling his dramatic reaction.

She had never been so eager, so unguarded, so wanton with a man before in all her life. It was as if another woman had taken over her body—a woman who felt beautiful and desired. A woman who had at long last met

her perfect match and now dared do anything to please
her man.

Clint kissed her deeply, his fingers swept aside the loose
edges of her robe and the straps of her nightgown so that
she was suddenly nearly bare to the waist. He stared down
at her for a moment, his blue eyes darkening with passion as he took in the sight of her golden red hair spread
out around her like a halo and her creamy white skin and
bare breasts, her dark nipples growing hard and erect under his gaze. He took her breasts in both his hands and
stroked her silky skin.

"You are absolutely gorgeous," he whispered as his
head dipped down to taste one taut nipple. At the sudden
erotic contact, Jessie shivered as a flash of heat rippled
through her body. His tongue swirled lazily around one
nipple, then moved to the next. Waves of heat like electricity simmered through her limbs. She moved her hips
restlessly against him as he pressed her breasts together
and his tongue moved between the throbbing peaks. Then
with roughened fingertips, he caressed and gently teased
her nipples. Jessie felt the honeyed heat gathering at the
core of her womanhood and she moved her hips against
him.

Her hands kneaded the hard muscles of his back and
moved down to the waistband of his jeans. She slipped her
hand between their bodies and managed to unhook his
belt and, finally, pull down the zipper of his jeans. As her
fingers stroked his rock-hard manhood, she felt his big
body shudder in her arms, his cheek rested again her bare
chest. Her hand wriggled slowly into his underwear and
she stroked his hard shaft.

Clint suddenly caught her by the wrist and rested his
cheek against her own.

"I want you, Jessie. More than I ever wanted anything in my life, I think. I'm just about to explode with wanting you." He rested his hand on top of hers and she felt the throbbing evidence of his desire. "But I need to be sure that's what you want, too."

In some distant part of her mind, she'd wondered at the wisdom of making love to him. Yet, her trepidation had hardly registered when matched against her desire. She'd never wanted a man so much in all her life and she simply didn't care about the consequences. If it was just this single time together, then so be it. She would savor and cherish every moment in his arms.

"I want to make love with you, Clint," she answered softly. As her fingers began to stroke him again, she gently kissed his cheek. "I want to feel you inside of me. Please, don't make me wait any longer—"

Clint needed no further assurances. He pressed a hard kiss to her mouth, then swiftly sat up and shed his shirt in one motion and his jeans, underwear and boots in another.

In the shadowy light, Jessie secretly treated herself to the sight of his naked body. Her gaze roamed hungrily over his stunning physique, his broad shoulders and muscular chest, covered with dark hair that tapered to a fine line over his flat stomach. She had only seconds however to commit the gorgeous sight of him to memory before he was close again, helping her slip her nightgown down her legs.

Jessie met his gaze and saw from the smoldering look in his eyes that he was experiencing the same thrill at the sight of her as she had known looking at him. His arms went around her instantly as he pulled her close and once again urged her to lie beneath him. Her arms encircled his shoulders and her legs wrapped around his lean hips. She ached with longing and anticipation. She wanted so badly to feel him inside of her, to capture him, yet at the same time, totally surrender to the mysterious power he had over her.

Their mouths met in a deep, soul-shattering kiss and Clint felt her warm and ready, burning him with her silken fire. This time, there was nothing between them but Clint's sincere desire to make their lovemaking as long and satisfying for Jessie as he could manage. His body's instinctive impulse was to join with her and move and move and move until he felt himself collapse, spent and exhausted in a heap of drained satisfaction. But in his heart, he had so many times imagined making love to this woman. And now, to hold her in his arms and feel her beneath him, joined with him in this way, was almost too good to be true. He wanted their lovemaking to surpass even his wildest fantasies. He wanted to urge her to heights of ecstasy that she had never imagined. He wanted to give her more pleasure than she'd ever known in the arms of a man.

She kissed him deeply and he moved against her, finally slipping slowly inside of her. Jessie gasped at the first shock of their joining and then seconds later, rocked her hips, urging him deeper and deeper. With a supreme effort at self-control, he moved within her, slowly at first, then harder and faster as Jessie moved beneath him, matching each powerful thrust of his hips, so responsive, so giving, so beautiful.

Jessie felt herself rocking on an ocean of desire, as wave after wave of heat washed over. As Clint moved inside of her, she felt her body melding with his, his hot, hard manhood driving deeper and deeper within her, eliciting sensations she had never felt before. Their lovemaking became harder, wilder, the tempo faster. She felt herself

opening to him completely, as if the floodgates to her very
soul had broken free. She held nothing back, giving herself totally and surrendering completely to the powerful
thrusts of his body and her own deep, building need for
release.

Jessie wished it could last forever, but finally, she felt
herself shatter in his arms, a sensation so sharp and sweet,
she cried out in ecstasy. Her body trembled as she reflex-
ively dug her nails into Clint's back and pressed her cheek
against his shoulder, the pleasure was so intense and pro-
longed. A white-hot spear of light darted through her,
leaving her shivering with pleasure again and again in its
wake.

Dropping small kisses on her moist forehead, Clint
pushed her still higher, gripping her hips with his hands as
he drove himself into her, lifting her to an unimaginable
height of pure white-hot ecstasy. He felt her tighten all
around him in the most intimate of passionate grips. Finally, he couldn't bear it any longer and simply let go, his
senses exploding with pleasure at his explosive climax.

His fierce cry of passion swelled Jessie's heart with satisfaction and the sound of her name murmured so lovingly was as sweet a sound as she'd ever heard. And one
Jessie knew she'd never forget.

Jessie woke in the early morning to the sound of Daisy's now-familiar cry. She was startled for a second by the
realization that she was naked. And, almost simultaneously, by the realization that she was not alone. Clint's
heavy, hair-covered arm was hooked around her waist and
his warm body curled around her, spoon-style. She felt his
chest hair tickling her back and at the curve of her bottom, sensations that confirmed his complete and utter
nakedness. Jessie slowly and gently disentangled herself,

allowing herself just a brief glance back at the bed to take in his glossy dark head on her pillow and his impressively muscular torso, bare to the waist. He looked so peaceful, like a gentle giant. As she watched him, he yawned in his sleep, tugged the covers up over his shoulder and rolled over.

She grabbed her robe off the rocking chair and pulled it on as she rushed to Daisy's room. It was all coming back now—she and Clint had made love. First on the couch. Then in her bed. Then in her bed, again. Unbelievable. But true.

She picked up Daisy, soothed her and quickly changed her diaper. Then she carried her into the kitchen and warmed up a bottle. "Oh, dear. What have I done?" Jessie asked Daisy.

The baby gurgled and patted Jessie's head. "Yes, baby. Dumb, dumb, dumb."

"What's so dumb?" Clint asked. He strolled into the room, his shirt open and his jeans hanging beltless on his hips. His hair was still mussed up and his cheeks showed a dark shadow of beard. He was a mess—and about the best-looking man Jessie had ever seen, anyplace, anytime.

"I was just thinking that I—I was out of coffee," Jessie stammered. "But then I realized that there's an extra can in the cupboard. I'll start a pot right after I feed Daisy." She tested the bottle on her wrist. It was ready and she sat down to let Daisy eat.

"I can fix the coffee," Clint said. "Just tell me where everything is."

A short time later, they sat face-to-face, sipping their coffee and trying to avoid meeting each other's gaze. It was one of the most awkward morning-after scenes Jessie could recall in her limited romantic experience. However, she had to note with some amusement that a baby in her lap sure supplied the perfect distraction.

Over the edge of his coffee mug, Clint guardedly sneaked glances at Jessie. She didn't have a stitch on under that robe and her efforts to keep the front modestly closed had only pulled the thin silky fabric tighter over her bare breasts, leaving nothing to the imagination. Clint sighed into his coffee as his gaze roamed over her. Her hair hung loose around her shoulders in a cloud of remarkable curls, the sight of it instantly bringing to mind the way it had looked last night, splayed out on the pillows around her head. He recalled the silky feel and lightly perfumed scent of it—the feel and scent of the woman herself, cleaved to his body in a passionate embrace, giving and receiving pleasure upon pleasure throughout the night. He had reveled in her natural sensuality, her responsiveness to his lovemaking and in the pleasure she had so generously given him in return.

He didn't know what she did to him, but it sure was something. Just thinking about the night they'd shared had him feeling hard and ready to return to bed, he reflected wryly. If she hadn't been holding Daisy, he would have acted on the impulse and swept Jessie up in his arms and carried her off to the nearest horizontal surface.

But first they had to talk. He had something important to say and now was as good a time as any to say it, he figured.

"I'm not exactly a morning person," Clint said suddenly. He gruffly cleared his throat. "I mean, I'm not a big talker in the morning."

No, he was not a big talker. He was a man of action. Jessie had always suspected as much and last night he had confirmed her suspicions, again and again.

"That's all right." She shrugged and rattled a set of plastic keys in front of Daisy. "I'm not much for conversation in the morning, either."

"But we do need to talk," he said quite firmly, this time catching her eye.

"Uh, what do we need to talk about?" Jessie asked. But even as she spoke the words, she had a sense of what was coming. This is where a guy like Clint decides he's going to do the honest and "up-front" thing and make it very clear that he is not in the market for any long-range attachments, commitments or responsibilities, she reflected.

As if she didn't already know that. As if she had any expectations about him. Any romantic illusions. As if she were in danger of falling in love with him. Jessie bit down on her lower lip.

The awful truth of the matter was that before he even showed up at her door last night, she was well on her way to falling for him. And last night, swept away on wave after wave of passion in his strong arms, Jessie had to wonder if she actually did love him. What other explanation could there be for these feelings? Had he felt it, even a little?

"I think we need to talk about what happened last night between us, for one thing," he said.

From his very tone and the way he nervously rubbed his hand along his jaw, Jessie had her answer. No, he hadn't felt a thing beyond pure, unbridled lust, and now he was going to try to politely talk his way out the door. If she didn't stop him, he'd start mumbling some halfhearted but thoroughly humiliating disclaimer for having made love to her.

Just as he had apologized for kissing her half-senseless on Christmas afternoon.

"Look, Clint, you don't have to explain or apologize for anything," Jessie said lightly. "Sometimes these things just...happen. We're two unattached adults. We're attracted to each other. And we acted on those feelings—"

"They just *happen*, huh?" he cut in. "Well, they don't just happen to me quite so easily," he said.

His sensitivity about her word choice was surprising, and stopped her short for a second. But, ignoring the look in his eyes, she continued. "I'm just trying to say that you don't have to worry. I don't have any...expectations," Jessie told him. "Isn't that what you're driving at?"

"If you would let me get a word in edgewise here, instead of trying to read my mind," he said through gritted teeth. "I wasn't going to apologize or explain about anything. I was about to ask you to marry me."

"Marry you?" Jessie shook her head. "What are you talking about?"

"You need a man to marry you, don't you? You told me so yourself last night," he pointed out. "Well—" He stared at her. She saw him swallow hard. "I think you should marry me."

"You think I should marry you," she echoed numbly. Of all the morning-after lines Jessie had anticipated, that was the last one she'd expected! Daisy had found a dangling curl irresistible and yanked hard, but Jessie didn't feel a thing.

"It would be the solution to all your problems," he assured her. "First of all, you'd have a husband guaranteed to do well in court in regard to the adoption. Second, I completely understand your needs for a temporary arrangement. You wouldn't be saddled with a man for longer than you needed one and there would be no hurt feelings on either side—" He cleared his throat again and looked her straight in the eyes. "And aside from all that, our sex life would be pretty darn spectacular. If last night was any indication."

Jessie felt her heart squeeze with a little pain. For a brief wonderful moment she had allowed herself to think that he might actually have some real feelings for her. Surely not love—she wasn't that fanciful. But feelings that were more than a mixture of neighborly friendship and pure lust. She let herself imagine that she'd finally gotten through to that rock Clint called a heart. But obviously she'd hit a bull's-eye somewhat lower on the man's anatomy.

"You're proposing to me just because we're good together in bed?" she asked him, her slowly simmering outrage beginning to rise.

"Now, that's not the only reason...." He paused and ran his hand through his hair. "You're also a damn good cook." He took a gulp of his coffee and shook his head. "Didn't you listen to a word I just said?" he replied in a frustrated tone.

"Well, you do expect a physical relationship as part of the deal. You aren't denying that, are you?"

"Why the hell should I deny it? After last night, how *could* I deny it?" he asked her. His point-blank look and the memories it evoked made Jessie blush. He jumped out of his seat and paced across the kitchen to the coffeepot. "Good chemistry between a man and a woman is as good a foundation for a marriage as anything else, in my opinion," he said gruffly as he filled his mug with coffee.

Jessie certainly disagreed with him there. She thought the only good foundation for marriage was love, the true and lasting kind. But she didn't have the energy, or the clarity of mind at that moment, to argue the point.

"For Christmas' sake, woman, I'm trying to help you out. I'm trying to do you a favor. You need a husband, don't you?'' He returned to the table and stared down at her. ''So what's wrong with me?''

What was wrong with him? *I'm probably in love with you and you don't care a fig about me! Not even after the way we made love last night,* she wanted to wail at him. *But aside from that tiny flaw, you're just perfect!*

''I can't marry you,'' Jessie blurted out. She set Daisy in her infant seat and gave her a rattle to play with. ''I mean, thanks for offering to help,'' she amended as she turned to face him, ''but I don't think it would work out very well. In fact, I know I'm sure it wouldn't.''

''Why in the world not?'' He stared at her, his dark brows knitted in an angry frown.

''It just... wouldn't. Take my word for it,'' she assured him.

''I deserve to hear a reason why you're so sure of that, don't I?'' he asked, his hands on his hips.

''Uh, I'm not sure I can explain it—'' Jessie stammered. ''We fight too much, for one thing. Why, every time we meet, we seem to find something to argue about.''

''We didn't argue much last night, as I recall,'' Clint pointed out.

Jessie looked at him, then down at the top of Daisy's head. She felt the warm color rising in her cheeks again. ''But we do have a way of just—well, disagreeing about everything. You have to admit that,'' she countered.

''We wouldn't disagree so much if you weren't so darn obstinate,'' he replied, taking a step closer. ''I'm offering a perfect solution to your problem and you're too damn stubborn to admit it. Why, you're the most hardheaded woman I've ever met in my entire—''

''Me, stubborn? Look who's talking!'' she replied in a tone of utter disbelief. ''Why, you can't even take a simple no for an answer.''

"Oh, is that so? Okay, I got the message, Jessie. If you don't want to marry me, I'm sure as hell not going turn myself inside out, trying to talk you into it," he said angrily. He stomped around the kitchen in his unlaced boots and Jessie followed him to the foyer, where he collected his jacket and hat.

"The answer is no, is it? Fine with me. Believe me, I won't bother you again," he shouted at her. With his shirt haphazardly buttoned, he hastily pulled on his jacket and hat and pulled open the front door. "Have a nice life—" he called over his shoulder.

Jessie stood in the open doorway, oblivious to the frosty morning air. "Clint?" she called out weakly after him. He didn't turn around. He got in his car, slammed the door closed and backed out of her driveway as if he'd just heard the starter's signal gun for the Indianapolis 500.

Jessie closed the door. A man proposed marriage to her—a man she probably loved—and she'd literally chased him out of her house. He wouldn't be back, either. Not after an exit like that one.

Not Clint.

Jessie turned to Daisy. "Oh, dear. What have I done?" she asked the little girl. In answer, Daisy could only offer her a set of colorful plastic keys.

When she reached the café with Daisy in tow a bit later that morning, Jessie didn't think she could feel any lower. She was hoping that the busy morning rush would take her mind off Clint. He had left his gun and holster at her house, she'd discovered, so it seemed pretty certain that she'd be in touch with him at least once more...and soon. But she wasn't at all sure what she should say when they met. Did she dare take him up on his offer? And what if he'd changed his mind about marrying her? That would be awfully embarrassing.

As Jessie mulled over her predicament, Alice entered the café and walked over to meet her. Alice greeted her and sat at the counter. From the expression on Alice's face, Jessie could tell instantly that it wasn't a mere social call.

She set a cup for coffee in front of her friend and filled it. "What's up, Alice?" Jessie asked bluntly.

"Jessie, you know I'm not the type to go prying into other people's business," Alice began, "but I heard some gossip this morning that I thought best to tell you about—"

"Gossip? About me, you mean?" Jessie asked. She laughed nervously. "About the personal-ad dates, I'd bet. Go on. I can stand it," she urged Alice.

"Yes, there's gossip about the ads," Alice said. "I've been meaning to speak to you about that. But it's not just the ads anymore, Jessie—" She signaled for Jessie to lean closer so that she could whisper. "I heard that Clint Bradshaw spent last night at your place."

Jessie gulped. She could feel the blood drain from her face. The speed at which news traveled in this town never failed to amaze her. "Who told you that?" she asked Alice quietly.

"Doesn't matter." Alice dismissed the question with a wave of her hand. "And quite frankly, who you choose to spend your time with is none of my business—or anyone else's," she added.

"I won't argue with that, Alice," Jessie said wryly. "Though most of the rest of the town obviously doesn't share your point of view."

"The problem is that Judge Hall is extremely conservative. You're going to have enough trouble with him as it is simply because you're single. If there's gossip flying around that portrays you as—" Here Alice paused,

searching for a suitably diplomatic expression that would
still get her point across.

"A loose woman?" Jessie supplied for her.

"Well, let's just say living less than a nunlike exis-
tence . . . ?" Alice replied. "And if you show up in court
with a husband you found in the personal ads and the
judge should find out, you won't have a chance of winning Daisy."

"I guess I was willing to try anything," Jessie explained. She hoped that Alice, her one ally, wasn't losing
faith in her fight to keep Daisy. "You don't think that the
judge has heard about it already, do you?" she hesitantly
asked.

"We can only hope he hasn't," Alice said soberly. "If
he has, I don't know what would remedy the situation—"

The bells on the café door jingled harshly and both
women turned to see Clint enter. He looked a bit better
than he had after stomping out of her house, Jessie noticed. Still, there was something not quite as crisp and neat
about his appearance as usual. Or maybe it was the dark
scowl on his face that gave her the impression that he was
feeling a bit off-key today.

He strode up to the counter and greeted Alice with a
brief nod. Then he looked straight at Jessie. He didn't say
hello, however.

"I left my gun at your house," he said to Jessie. Alice,
who was trying not to listen in, suddenly made a soft
choking sound on her coffee. Clint looked over at her.
"Yes, Alice, I know Freud would have a field day with
that one."

"I think I'll go make a phone call to my office," Alice
said, trying to slip away with a polite excuse.

"Uh, don't go yet, Alice," Jessie stammered. She rested her hand lightly on Clint's arm, drawing his curious stare. She took the fact that he didn't remove her hand as a good sign and gamely forged ahead. "I was just about to tell you some wonderful news—"

"What wonderful news was that, Jessie?" Clint asked in a low, grating tone.

"Oh, don't be shy, honey. We can tell Alice," she replied in a honey-sweet voice. A voice that made the tips of his toes tingle inside his boots.

She glanced up at him briefly, a flicker in his eye telling her that he had caught on to her act. Or was that the flicker of anger rekindled from this morning's argument? Jessie licked her lips, not daring to glance up at him again as she edged herself a tiny bit closer.

"Alice—Clint and I are engaged to be married."

"You are?" Alice looked shocked and delighted. "Why didn't you tell me sooner?"

"We, uh, we wanted to keep things a secret until we figured out all the details," Jessie stammered. "It all happened so suddenly, I guess we're still getting used to the idea ourselves."

Now she had to look at Clint. This was the deciding moment. Either he was going to hang her out to dry—or he was going to be a good sport about the whole thing, take up his oar and start rowing like crazy.

She slowly raised her gaze to meet his, terrified of what she'd find there.

Six

___

Clint stared down into Jessie's wide brown eyes. Two hours ago, he had promised himself that he'd never willingly come within a mile of the woman unless it had to do with an official police emergency. That was before he'd realized he'd run out of her place without his gun. Okay, he'd get the gun and that would be the end of it.

Driving over to the café and feeling calmer, he'd realized she had let him off a pretty darn big hook by refusing his proposal. With a clear head, he didn't understand how he had ever proposed marriage to her in the first place. His hormones had gotten so stirred up by their night of lovemaking, he'd lost his mind. That had to be the only explanation for it.

His pride had been stung by her flat-out refusal, for sure. Especially since it seemed as if she were willing to marry any man who could fog a mirror. But he had

breathed a mighty sigh of relief thinking about the matrimonial bullet he'd dodged.

But now that matrimonial shotgun was pointed at him
again. And fired from point-blank range. He knew he
could duck. He had every right to. And it would serve her
right for the way she'd turned him down this morning.

Here was his chance to show her that Clint Bradshaw
didn't take that kind of treatment from any woman.

Clint stared down in Jessie's pleading eyes, prepared to
do just that.

But he couldn't.

Just as it always seemed to happen with her, everything in his mind got confused. Except for the overriding
impulse to stand by her, to protect her, to do what he
could to help her.

"Well," he said slowly, "I guess the secret is out." He
slipped his arm around Jessie's shoulder and turned to
look at Alice. "Time to face the music, honey," Clint
said, squeezing Jessie's shoulder just a tiny bit tighter than
was necessary.

"Yes, I guess it's time," she agreed, smiling up at him
with a look that was a mixture of relief, gratitude and
distraction at being held so close to his big warm body.

Alice gushed. "Let me be the first to congratulate you
two. What wonderful news."

Before Alice could ask any more tricky questions about
the "secret" engagement, Sophie abandoned her customers to see what all the excitement was about.

"What news?" Sophie asked, hustling over. She
quickly took in Clint standing with his arm around Jessie. "You two split a winning lottery ticket or something?"

"We're getting married, Sophie," Clint told her.

"Married!" She gasped and pressed both hands to her round cheeks. "Let me sit down a minute...." She took a deep breath and Jessie quickly passed her a glass of water and fanned her face with a menu. "Oh my goodness...who would have thought it?" She stared at Jessie first, and then Clint. "The two of you...all this time...I didn't suspect a thing...."

"Your order is up, old woman," Charlie groused at Sophie as he stormed out of the kitchen. "Folks want to eat their food hot, you know."

"Oh, hush up. Jessie and Clint—they're getting married!" Sophie shouted back. "What do you think of that!"

"Is that all?" He shook his head and waved a metal cooking spoon at her. "I could've told you that pot was about to boil over," he grumbled as he wandered back into the kitchen. "Why, anybody with eyes in his head could see that young fella has it bad. And she's been no better...just about walking into walls around here..." he chattered on to no one in particular.

As the clanging of pots and pans covered over Charlie's muttering, everyone looked at Clint and Jessie. Clint stared down at his boot and rubbed his ear. Jessie coughed and smoothed her hair with her hand.

"I guess I'd better be going," Alice said. "Congratulations again, you two. I couldn't be happier for you," she said as she waved goodbye.

"Oh, this is such wonderful news." Sophie rose up from her chair and wiped her eyes with her apron. She hugged first Jessie and then Clint to her ample figure. "I've just got to tell everyone I know," she said brightly, and without waiting for the consent of the engaged couple, she trotted off to do exactly that.

Suddenly left alone on their own, Clint looked down at Jessie. With his hands resting on her shoulders, he turned her so that she was forced to face him. "I hope you're sure of what you're doing," he said in a low tone. "With all these witnesses, you won't be able to get out of this so easily."

"Then I guess we're stuck with each other," Jessie said. She took a deep breath and twisted away from him. A temporary marriage to Clint was going to be hard for her—but for exactly the opposite reasons than he suspected.

He didn't answer. But he didn't move away, either. He just remained standing a bit too close for Jessie's comfort, gazing down at her thoughtfully, looking every inch the anxious groom, unable to take his eyes off his bride-to-be.

Jessie's curt reply hadn't exactly pumped up his ego. Yet he felt a certain undeniable happiness welling up inside. He was going to make this woman his wife. And—even more importantly—no other man was going to have her.

It seemed best to both Jessie and Clint to get the marriage over with as quickly as possible. They decided on Sunday, just five short days after the announcement of their engagement. When Jessie told Clint about her conversation with Alice, they both thought it would be best if everyone continued to believe that the marriage was a love match, and not just a temporary deal cooked up to help with the adoption. Therefore, though their arrangements were hasty, for the sake of appearances, they thought they ought to comply with at least the minimum of wedding customs.

They arranged to be married at a local church. The guest list was short, and included only Jessie's café crew, Alice and her husband, and, of course, Daisy. Clint asked one of his deputies to be his witness and Jessie asked Sophie. Jessie was sorry that her aunt would be unable to attend. Even though it wasn't a real marriage, Jessie believed that this would be Claire's last chance to see her at the altar. After being married to Clint, Jessie knew she would never meet another man she'd want to share her life with.

Clint's brother and sister couldn't make it either on such short notice, but sent all their best wishes and promised to visit soon.

Although Jessie knew in her heart that she wasn't a real bride, for some strange reason she felt like one. It was easy to succumb to the fantasy, with Ivy and Sophie fussing over her constantly, asking about her wedding dress, how she would fix her hair and what type of flowers did she have in mind for a bouquet. One afternoon, they even surprised Jessie with a tiny shower—just the two waitresses and Alice Hoag. When Jessie unwrapped their gift—an obscenely expensive and ridiculously sheer nightgown and robe set made of lavender silk—she blushed as bright as any true bride.

She bought herself a new dress—forest green velvet trimmed with black satin piping, with a low scoop neckline, a long skirt and a short jacket that fitted tightly at the waist. And she bought a new dress for Daisy, as well—a tiny red velvet smock with a beautiful lace collar.

Since Clint rented a small apartment, it only made sense that he would move into Jessie's house. As she cleaned out a closet and a chest of drawers for Clint's belongings, it suddenly struck her how little she really knew about the man she was about to marry.

She knew he liked to argue . . . and she knew he liked to make love. That was all she knew for sure. And it would have to be enough, she reflected. After agreeing on the arrangements, Jessie had seen little of her fiancé for the rest of the week. She thought he might arrive on her doorstep some night. And she would have surely taken him in. But he never appeared.

Jessie wondered about his distant attitude all week. By Saturday night, she wondered about it even more. Maybe he was getting cold feet, she thought, as she painted her rather stubby nails with pale pink polish. Her hands shook a bit from nerves, making the polish go on in wavy lines. It wouldn't be the first time a man had reconsidered a proposal of marriage. Jessie knew that only too well.

The phone rang, a sharp sound in the otherwise silent house. Jessie jumped, startled by the sound. She picked up the phone, surprised to hear Clint's voice on the other end.

"Clint? Is something wrong?" Jessie asked him.

"Why should anything be wrong?" He laughed at her. "I just wanted to speak to my bride the night before the wedding. It isn't bad luck or anything to just call, is it?"

It unnerved her to hear him talking to her as if their wedding was for real. Wasn't this the way lovers spoke to each other? Not the way a man who was marrying a woman "to do her a favor" or just because "they were good in bed" should be talking.

"It's late and I didn't expect to hear from you," she explained.

"You sound as if you're nervous, Jessie," he said in a softer tone. "You're not nervous about marrying me, are you?"

"Me, nervous? Of course not," she scoffed. She was thankful that he couldn't hear her heart beating like a drum through the phone line.

"I thought you might be getting cold feet," he said quietly. "You're not having second thoughts about marrying me, are you?"

"Is that why you called, Clint?" she answered slowly. "To find out if I was going to stand you up tomorrow?"

"No, not at all," he replied. "I just wanted you to know that when you get to the church tomorrow, I'll be waiting for you."

His words and the soft, warm tone of his voice touched her heart. Somehow Clint had guessed her secret fear. He had guessed the private nightmare that would have been keeping her awake all night. Sam Kincaid had told her that he loved her, but he had failed her and deeply hurt her. Clint Bradshaw had never spoken one word about love, but he'd made her a promise and he wanted her to know that he would be true to his word.

"Clint—" Jessie was nearly moved to tears and could hardly speak. "Thank you," she said simply.

"You're welcome," he replied. From his very tone, she could envision the soft smile on his handsome face. "Sleep well, Jessie. We have a big day tomorrow."

"I will," she replied and meant it. "Good night, Clint."

He wished her good-night and hung up the phone. Jessie hung up, as well, and sat quietly for a long time, thinking about him. She did love him. She knew that now, and it was a relief to admit it to herself freely. She wanted to marry him and be his wife for however long it lasted. Her heart would break when their time together was over, but Jessie was willing to pay that price. At least she'd have Daisy to console her. And it was better to be married to

Clint for a few months, she reasoned, than to some other man for fifty years.

Clint knew full well that Jessie was a beautiful woman. It should only logically follow that she would be a beautiful bride. He had expected as much. Yet, when he caught sight of her walking down the aisle toward him, for the first time in his life he felt genuinely faint. She was, in every sense of the word, a breathtaking vision, from the halo of flowers in her upswept hair to the hem of her flowing, emerald green velvet skirt.

The church was decorated with white satin ribbons, pine boughs and white candles. Jessie held a small bouquet of white roses and tiny orchids. Clint could smell their sweet perfume as she came up and stood beside him. He faced her and looked down into her beautiful upturned face. He heard the minister's words, off at a far distance, although the man was standing right beside him. He sensed other people around, yet he saw only his radiant bride.

When the time came, he took her soft, cool hand in his own. In a strong, clear voice he repeated the vows, staring deeply into her eyes as he said the words. She did the same to him, her words penetrating to his very soul—"to have and to hold, to honor and cherish, in sickness and his health, in good time and in bad, until death do us part." She slipped the plain gold band on his finger. He clasped her hand and held it tight.

The minister pronounced them man and wife. "You may kiss the bride," he said.

Clint leaned over and kissed her—the sweetest, most perfect kiss of his life. He knew he'd surprised her; he felt her cling to him, her soft lips melting under his own. The sound of the minister clearing his throat brought him back to his senses.

The minister gave them a final blessing. "Congratulations," he said. Clint managed to give the minister a handshake with his left hand while still holding Jessie's hand with his right. Clint led his bride down the aisle, feeling as if his feet never touched the ground. Outside the church, the small wedding party pelted them with about ten pounds of birdseed.

Although they had planned to go straight to Jessie's house, it seemed that Sophie and the others had cooked up other plans. "I know you newlyweds are eager to be alone, but you just have to come back to the café for a few minutes," Sophie said.

"We have a wedding cake for you, and champagne," Ivy said.

"Folks want to wish you well, you know," Charlie chimed in.

"Folks?" Jessie echoed. She glanced over at Clint. "What folks?"

"Just folks." Charlie shrugged. The others looked at him, shaking their heads. He had obviously given something away.

"Do you mind?" Jessie asked Clint.

"Of course not," Clint said. "They must have arranged some sort of party for us. It wouldn't be polite if we didn't go."

When they arrived at the café the rest of town was there to greet them. There was a big banner congratulating the happy couple, and paper streamers and balloons. Clint and Jessie had a second shower, this time of confetti. A huge wedding cake and other edibles were set out on the counter as a buffet. Charlie had outdone himself and cooked up his specialties—platters of fried chicken and mashed potatoes, three-alarm chili and a huge lasagna.

As the party rolled along, Sophie pushed the tables back to make a dance floor. Charlie had rigged up the jukebox so that it didn't need any quarters and supplied an eclectic but steady mix of music.

Everyone wanted to take a turn dancing with the bride and bouncing the baby on their knee. It was not quite the reception that Jessie had imagined for her "someday" wedding. Yet, she had never danced more, laughed more or was hugged and kissed by more friends at a party in her life. She could not recall a more joyful day—and she felt blessed by the sincere good wishes of everyone who knew her.

She had been wrong to think that people were waiting to see if Clint would turn tail and run, as Sam as done. She was wrong to think badly of her neighbors and friends. They didn't wish her any ill. They clearly wished her only happiness. Maybe Sam Kincaid had taken away more than her pride; he had stolen her ability to trust, and her natural inclination to think the best of people, not the worst. But because of Clint, all that had changed.

Finally it was time for the bride and groom to go home. Alice had insisted on baby-sitting for Daisy overnight so that Jessie and Clint could have at least one honeymoon night alone. For the sake of appearances, Jessie had agreed and thanked her for the favor.

All week she had wondered if Alice suspected that the marriage wasn't real. After all, she was the one who had suggested to Jessie that she find a man willing to work out a deal. Since Alice was helping her so much with the adoption, Jessie thought she should tell her the truth. On the morning of the wedding, when Alice and her husband, Dan, came to pick Jessie up for church, Jessie thought she would confess. And she almost did, too, when Alice came into her bedroom to help her finish dressing.

But before she had worked up the nerve, Alice said, "I'm so glad that you and Clint decided to get married. You don't know how my conscience bothered me after I suggested that you get involved in some sort of fake arrangement. It was totally unethical of me. I might have even lost my job if anyone found out. But now I don't have to worry. This marriage certainly came at a convenient time, but you and Clint are so head over heels about each other, no one would ever imagine that it wasn't true love."

Jessie just smiled and pretended to fuss with the hem of her dress. Now that she knew how Alice had worried, she couldn't burden her with the truth. Even if it made her feel better to share the secret with a friend.

"Now, don't you worry about Daisy," Alice assured Jessie and Clint as they got ready to leave the party. "She'll be just fine with Dan and me. Won't you, sweetheart?"

Jessie kissed Daisy's cheek and handed her over to Alice, who already had the baby's diaper bag and other essentials in hand.

"Ready to go?" Clint said grimly. He stood by her side, his big hand clasped possessively on her elbow. Jessie nodded and they made their way through the throng of well-wishers, and out the front door of the café. As the door closed behind them, Jessie heard the bells jingle. It was snowing outside, just as it had been on Christmas Eve night, and as Clint helped Jessie into his car, she thought of the first time she had ever set eyes on him. It seemed so long ago, yet it had been only a few weeks. That very first moment she had seen him, she had felt so many things, so many thoughts and impressions had run through her mind. Yet she had never expected to be married to him.

She glanced at her husband's rugged profile, her gaze dropping to the steering wheel and the gold band on the ring finger of his left hand. She sat back in her seat and stared out her window. They were well and truly married. It was the first quiet moment she'd had all day to reflect upon what she had done, and the enormity of it suddenly took her breath away.

Clint pulled the car up the driveway of Jessie's house and as she opened her door to let herself out, he came around to help her.

"You can't go tramping through the snow in those shoes," he said, looking down at her velvet pumps. "They'll be ruined."

"Well I can't very well fly up the walk," Jessie said, gathering up her skirt so that the hem wouldn't drag in the snow. "I should have brought my boots along I guess, but I thought they'd squeak too loud when I walked up the aisle to the altar. You know, ruin the mood," she said.

"I don't know why that should have bothered you, Jessie," Clint said, laughing at her. "You seem to wear those darn boots with everything else. Why not a wedding dress?"

And before she knew what was happening, he scooped her up in his arms and began carrying her up the walk.

"Clint—what are you doing?" she protested. "Put me down! You'll hurt yourself—"

"Stop squawking, woman," Clint replied. "Or I'll toss you over my shoulder in a fireman's hold and then you'll really have something to complain about."

They had reached her front porch, but Clint still didn't release her. "Put me down. This instant," she insisted. She tried to wriggle free of his hold, but he only tightened his grip. Though she had admired his impressive physique, she'd never realized how strong he was. He held her close in a steely grip that made it almost impossible to breathe, much less wiggle loose.

"Give me your key," he commanded.

Then she realized what was happening. "You are not carrying me over the threshold . . . that's just plain silly."

"Forget it. I bet I can guess where you hide the spare one," he grumbled, and with his elbow he nudged aside a flowerpot on the ledge beside the door. Sure enough, there was the spare key to Jessie's house. He plucked it up with one hand and deftly opened the door.

Jessie felt herself swung through the doorway in Clint's strong arms. "Here we are, bride. Safe and sound and following all the traditions," he told her.

Finally, in the dark foyer, he slowly set her on her feet. He was breathing a bit heavily, partly from the exercise and partly from holding in his laughter. Jessie's hold on him was awkward and as her high-heeled shoes came to the floor, she clung to his shoulders just to keep her balance. By now, she was laughing, too.

As her slim body slid seductively down the hard length of his, she felt his cheek pressed to her warm neck and then his lips hungrily moving over her warm skin. She relaxed in his arms and her head fell back, exposing the creamy white column of her throat. Their laughter melted into moans of pleasure as their lips met in a smoldering kiss.

Jessie's hands quickly pushed Clint's coat off his shoulders and it fell to the floor. Her fingers next moved to his tie and undid the knot, then slipped open the buttons of his suit jacket and shirt. While Clint's lips moved over hers with mesmerizing kisses, he removed her coat and the small velvet jacket she wore over her dress. His mouth moved lower, tasting the silky skin that swelled from the low neckline of her dress, his hands moving sensuously over her velvet bodice, cupping her breasts and massaging their tingling peaks. Jessie's head spun and her legs wobbled beneath her.

She felt Clint's strong arm encircle her waist just in time. She pulled her mouth from his and took a deep breath, then pressed her head to his shoulder. His hand moved to her lower back and he gently pressed her into the heat of his lower body. "I carried you across the threshold, bride. What's next on the list of wedding-night traditions, do you think?" he growled against her ear.

"Well, I don't think we need to make love in the threshold," Jessie managed to murmur. "I think simply transporting me over it was sufficient."

"Mmm—" Clint moaned thoughtfully as he rocked her against his hardened body. Jessie clung to him. She felt as if she were simply melting against him. She'd never been with a man who could make her want him so much so quickly. "No making love in the threshold, eh? How about the bedroom?"

"I suppose that would be in keeping with tradition...." Jessie sighed.

"Too far...." Clint groaned. Jessie silently agreed. The bedroom seemed light-years away from where they stood. She took his hand and led him a few short steps into the living room.

In a distant part of her mind, she realized that her expensive bridal-shower nightgown would have to sit wrapped in tissue paper for at least another night.

She stood in front of the couch and held both of Clint's hands in her own. She looked up into his deep blue eyes. Only the light from the porch filtered into the darkened room, but it was enough for her to see the passion smoldering in the smoky blue depths of his eyes.

"I want you so much," he confessed. "I think I'll just die if I don't take you this instant...."

Jessie's answering sigh almost put him over the edge. He groaned and pulled her close. For the past five days, Clint had been able to think of little else, except making love to Jessie again. His body was rock hard and ready. When she smoothed his shirt off his arms and undid the buckle of his belt, he felt as if he were about to explode.

He kissed her deeply and pulled her down to the couch. They tumbled across the pillows with Clint seated and Jessie stretched out across his lap. While he still was kissing her, his hands moved under her skirt and down the length of her legs as he pulled off her panty hose and panties. His fingertips grazed the wet, honeyed center of her femininity. As he stroked her lovingly, she gripped his shoulders, shuddering with passion. She was more than ready for him and her passionate response made him lose his last shred of control.

In one swift movement, he pushed down his pants and pulled her across his lap. Her thighs spread open and he thrust himself inside her. Jessie gripped Clint's shoulder and fitted herself even closer to him, eager to feel him sink into her velvety heat. She moved with him as he thrust himself within her.

Once. Twice. And then a third time.

White-hot lights exploded in her mind's eye as she instantly reached a peak of sensual ecstasy. Her body pulsated and shuddered, her head dropping limply to his shoulder.

"Jessie...." he whispered with his mouth pressed to her hair. "Stay with me, honey. The best is yet to come...."

Just when Jessie didn't think she could bear a moment's more pleasure, Clint rocked inside of her, slowly but surely teasing and tempting her to another astounding peak. He had pulled down the bodice of her dress to expose the hardened tips of her breasts, and his mouth moved warmly over one nipple. Electricity wildly danced up and down her limbs as his mouth and fingers did wicked and wonderful things to her.

Jessie answered his sensuous assault by covering Clint's face and neck with kisses as her fingers tangled in the dense dark hair on his chest. She dipped her head and twirled her tongue around one flat male nipple. He groaned with delight as his hips bucked up, pushing his manhood deeper inside of her.

Without their bodies separating from their intimate tangle, Clint hugged her close and moved around so that she was suddenly beneath him. Holding himself up on his forearms, he stared down into her eyes. He touched her hair with his fingertips.

"My beautiful bride," he whispered, as he moved inside of her again. Jessie closed her eyes and gripped him close, wrapping her legs tightly around his slim waist as she matched his rhythm with the sensuous movement of her hips.

He drove them higher and higher, until Jessie felt herself shattering again into a million flaming fragments. Seconds later, in one powerful thrust she felt Clint reach his own peak. His body shuddered against her as he cried out in pure pleasure. He sank down on top of her, his damp forehead pressed against her bare shoulder.

They lay together without either one moving a muscle for a long time. Jessie thought Clint had fallen asleep.

Then she felt his head stir, his thick silky hair tickling her nose.

In a deep, raspy voice he whispered, "You know, I think I'm going to like being married."

Jessie softly laughed. "I'm going to like it, too."

Seven

——

True to her first impression, married life with Clint was full of unimaginable delights. And more than a few of them involved her husband's masterful lovemaking. It seemed the more they had of each other, the more they wanted, and when Jessie slipped under the covers each night, she found Clint eager to lead her to the ever-new and greater heights of passion.

But there was more between them than a physical relationship—or her good cooking. Every day Jessie learned more about Clint, and felt herself falling deeper and deeper in love with him. He was a difficult and stubborn man, to be sure. She knew that much going in. But there was a gentle and tender side to him that he had only allowed her to glimpse from time to time. Now, as he permitted his armor to slip just a notch or two, she was able to see so much more of him.

She couldn't think about the time when the adoption was finalized and their marriage would end. And she soon stopped reminding herself that Clint didn't really love her and had only married her out of a combination of some misplaced sense of gentlemanly conduct—and sheer lust.

The only way Jessie could live from day to day with her new husband was to pretend that they would share a life together forever.

They were married about two weeks when Jessie woke up one night to find herself alone in bed. She glanced at the clock. It was half past two. Then she heard Daisy softly whimpering. She quickly rose out of bed and pulled her robe on over her nightgown.

She found Clint in Daisy's nursery, cradling the baby to his chest as he walked up and down the length of the room. He looked up at Jessie when she entered. "She's having a little trouble falling back to sleep. Maybe she's hungry."

"I'll get her a bottle," Jessie said. She went down to the kitchen, heated a bottle and brought it back upstairs. Clint was sitting in the rocker with Daisy cradled in his arms. Jessie heard him humming softly to her as the chair rocked to and fro.

"There, there, sweet girl. Sweet little Emily," Jessie heard him say. "Don't cry, Emily. Daddy's here."

She stood very still, not knowing what to do. Had she heard him correctly? No, she was sure of it. He had said, "Emily." She had always sensed some mystery in his past that he deftly avoided speaking of. A mystery that she guessed somehow involved a child.

Up until tonight, Clint had acted in a paternal and protective way towards Daisy, but had still kept his distance. Although he always treated her tenderly, he was reluctant, Jessie had noticed, to play with her or even give her a bottle. When she cried in the night, he had never once even offered to go to her like this. Jessie didn't quite understand it. He obviously knew a lot about children. Could he know so much and still feel awkward or clumsy... or even afraid of a baby like Daisy?

Now, here was another piece to the puzzle. Emily. Did she dare ask him about it?

Clint rose and gently placed Daisy in her crib. He carefully tucked the blankets around her, then leaned over and softly kissed her cheek. Jessie left the baby's room and Clint followed.

"I guess she didn't need that bottle after all," he whispered to her. Jessie glanced down at the bottle of formula she was holding. She'd nearly forgotten about it.

"I think she'll sleep now," she said. The hallway was dark and Jessie couldn't see his face clearly. She walked beside him to their room where he switched on the lamp beside the bed. She sat down beside him on the bed and took his hand.

"Clint—" She didn't know how to ask him about what she had heard, but she had to know the truth. "When you were putting Daisy to sleep... you called her Emily."

He stared at her. "I did?"

Jessie somberly nodded. She looked down at his hand, gripped in both of her own. "You called her Emily... and then you said, 'Don't cry, Emily. Daddy's here.'" She looked up at him. "Do you have a daughter, Clint, named Emily?"

She saw the blood drain from his face as he abruptly came to his feet. He turned away from her so that she could no longer see his face, only his broad bare back, the muscles bunched and tense, his fists clenched at his sides.

"I don't want to talk about this now, Jessie. I think I'm going to take a walk. Get some air."

He pulled open the closet and pulled out a sweatshirt. Jessie got up and stood in front of him. "Don't just run out on me like this, Clint. We need to talk...."

He pulled the sweatshirt over his head and glared at her. "There's nothing to talk about, Jessie. I..." He paused and stared at her. The gray-blue depths of his eyes were filled with pain. As Jessie stared into his eyes, she felt as if her heart were about to break. "I need to go out. I need to walk. Just let me go." His voice was low and strained. If Jessie didn't know him better, she might have been afraid of him.

"No—" Jessie gripped his arm. She knew that with his strength, he could have easily shaken her off. But he didn't. "Just talk to me, Clint. Tell me about Emily. Please?" she practically begged him.

I love you so much, she wanted to say. *I'd do anything to erase that pain from your eyes. Please let me help you.*

But she couldn't say that. Instead, she just held on to his arm and looked straight into his eyes. Finally she felt his body relax a bit under her touch. He looked down at her, his expression harsher and darker than she'd ever seen, his features looking as if they'd been etched in stone.

"I *had* a little girl name Emily once," he said. "She died in a car accident when she was four years old. I guess holding Daisy reminded me...." His voice trailed off in a heart-wrenching sob of grief.

He sat on the bed and covered his face with his hands. Jessie sat beside him and put her arms around him. She felt his body shake as he cried. Jessie stroked his back and his hair. She whispered lovingly to him. She touched her fingertips to her eyes and realized that she was crying, too.

She understood so many things now. Why he was so distant, yet kind to Daisy. How he knew so much about babies. Why he was so guarded, so seemingly unfeeling at times. Why he seemed so wary of making a commitment to a woman, or having a family. He had been hurt so badly. Maybe he couldn't bear the idea of starting all over again. When Jessie thought about it, it now seemed amazing that he had even agreed to their temporary marriage.

Yet, as all of these questions were answered, a flock of new mysteries sprung up to replace them. Who was Emily's mother? Had Clint been married to her?

Finally he sat up and wiped his eyes with the back of his hands. "I haven't cried for years—I'm sorry," he said softly.

"You have nothing to apologize for," Jessie replied. "I'm so sorry about your daughter."

"I suppose I should have told you about it," he said. He stood up and paced to the other side of the room. "Maybe that wasn't right. It happened about five years ago. I try not to think about her."

"Of course," Jessie said. "I understand."

"I guess I should tell you everything now, Jessie." He turned to face her. "I was married once before. Her name was Glory. Sort of a stage name, you might say, short for Gloria," he explained with a slightly derisive tone.

After hearing about his daughter, she couldn't say the news was a total shock. Yet, hearing him give a name to some faceless wife did give Jessie an unexpected jolt.

"She was Emily's mother?" Jessie asked.

"Yes, Glory was Emily's mother," he echoed. Jessie noticed that he twisted the gold band on his finger as he spoke. He took a deep breath and continued.

While Jessie patiently listened he explained how he had met Glory while he was training to be a police officer. He was very young and inexperienced with women. She was a secretary who did a little modeling on the side. She wanted to be an actress and he thought she was incredibly glamorous. They'd barely known each other a month when she told him she was pregnant. He proposed marriage on the spot. He was head over heels in love with her—or so he thought—and he was thrilled to make her his wife.

This part of the story caused Jessie a silent stab of pain. His first courtship had certainly been different from their own, she reflected. Why, he had offered to marry her in the same tone a boyfriend might offer to... well, wash your car. As a manly sort of favor to a lady in need. She stifled a sigh. She couldn't imagine a man *less* swept off his feet by a woman than Clint had been by her. In comparison to his feelings about Glory, she guessed she came in a very distant second.

But the marriage was rocky from the start, he continued. Glory had enjoyed being pursued, but she found actual marriage too dull for her tastes. Once she had the baby, she concentrated on getting her figure back and planning her escape to Hollywood. She was still determined to be a star, Clint told Jessie.

"While Glory was training for stardom—taking acting and singing classes and buying clothes by the truckload, I cared for Emily. I was working nights and we certainly couldn't afford a full-time sitter while Glory was out all day," he explained.

As Jessie guessed, they soon divorced. With a pained expression on his face once more, Clint explained how he had fought in court for custody of his daughter. Glory was an uncaring, neglectful mother. She didn't even know Emily's daily routine, or her favorite toys and TV shows. Yet, the court still granted Glory custody of Emily. She took Emily to California, however, in violation of the

custody agreement. Clint went back to court and fought
to get his daughter back.

"I think I would have won, too," he said quietly. "The
accident occurred only a week before the hearing. Glory
was in the car, as well. A boyfriend of hers was driving.
They'd both been drinking. Neither of them was seriously hurt," he added. He cleared his throat. "Only Emily."

Jessie didn't know what to say. She had so much to
think about. She stared down at her hands, clasped tightly
in her lap.

"Thank you for telling me all this, Clint. I know it
wasn't easy for you," she said.

"I guess I've wanted to tell you for a while. I just didn't
know how. But now you know everything...." His voice
trailed off.

*You know why I can't stay here with you and Daisy and
be your husband for real,* he wanted to say. *You know why
I can never give you what you need, Jessie. Maybe if I had
met you first, sweetheart, my life would have turned out
differently. But we can't change the past—and sometimes, no matter what we wish, we can't escape the damage life works on us.*

He met Jessie's questioning gaze and then reached out
and cupped her cheek with the palm of his hand.

"When I felt so bad before... and you put your arms
around me..." He paused and looked away. Jessie
thought he might start crying again, but he quickly re-
gained his self-control. "The thing I'm trying to say is,
when it happened, there was no one around to talk to," he
continued. "No family or friends, I mean.... Until tonight, I was alone with it for a long time."

Jessie didn't know what to say. She would be there for
him for as long as he needed her. Forever and a day, if he

wanted her. She took his hand and led him back to their bed.

"We've talked enough for tonight, don't you think? Let's go back to bed," she said quietly.

He pulled off his sweatshirt and then kicked off his jeans. In an instant, he was in bed beside her under the covers. He flicked off the lamp and pulled her close. She slipped her arms around his waist and rested her cheek on his bare chest. She felt his lips on her hair.

"You're so good to me, Jessie," he whispered. "Sometimes I don't think I deserve it. I know I don't."

His first kiss was so tender that Jessie thought her heart would break. Their kisses mingled with their tears, one kiss and one touch leading to another until their love-making quickly caught fire. And although she had reached the heights of passion many times before in his arms, Jessie had never before felt so close to him, as if an invisible wall that had always separated them had suddenly crumbled.

She didn't fool herself into believing that Clint loved her, but she felt as if perhaps he finally trusted her, and had allowed her just a few precious steps closer to his heart.

After that night, she noticed that he treated Daisy differently, too. He was no longer a protective, but distant presence in Daisy's life, but an honest-to-goodness, hands-on dad. Whenever Jessie needed a helping hand with Daisy's care, Clint stepped right in. He was now willing to feed her, bathe her, change her diapers and make funny faces and wacky animal noises to entertain her for hours on end.

Sometimes, watching him down on the floor with Daisy as they played together, Jessie actually felt tears well up in her eyes. He was the perfect father for her little girl—

kind, strong and endlessly patient. Did he ever think about staying with them? she wondered. Did he ever daydream, as she did, about making their "arrangement" a real family? The way she did....

Marriage and motherhood definitely agreed with Jessie. During the first weeks as a newly married bride, everyone in town had some compliment or comment to bestow. She really "glowed," Sophie said. She had "a lot of bounce for the ounce," Charlie observed. Married life had made Jessie a "new woman," Mrs. Ogilvy at the bank said with a sly wink one morning.

Jessie even looked different and began wearing her hair in a new, loose and curly style. And instead of hiding her slender figure under layers of comfortable, but baggy old clothes, she began paying a bit more attention to her wardrobe. Ivy was a great help there, advising Jessie on the hottest new styles—and giving her the courage to wear them. Whenever Jessie felt self-conscious in a new outfit, she checked out what she privately called the "Clint meter." He never said much, but a certain sparkle in his eyes told her that he definitely approved of her look. And if the Clint meter really registered high ... well, Jessie began to expect more than a mere look in response.

Each time she and Clint made love it was more wonderful than the last. And each time he joined his body to hers in a passionate embrace, Jessie could swear that he loved her truly and would never leave her or their baby. Then morning's light would come and she would have to face the sad fact that though she loved Clint with all her heart, he would never return those feelings.

They were married about a month when Alice Hoag delivered the news to Jessie and Clint one afternoon in the café that Judge Hall wanted to interview the newlyweds.

Privately. In his chambers. The next day at nine o'clock sharp.

"He wants to *interview* us?" Jessie practically squeaked. "More like interrogate us, don't you think?"

"Now, don't get all stressed, Jessie. He just wants to ask you and Clint a few questions in a more informal setting than the courtroom," Alice replied.

Clint had stopped by the café for lunch and sat at the counter calmly eating a turkey and Swiss cheese sandwich. He didn't look too worried, Jessie noticed.

"I know that wily old dog, Hall," Clint said finally. He wiped his mouth with a napkin and hopped down from his seat. "He just wants to poke around, see if the marriage is for real. I hear he's still pretty sharp, too," he added.

"Clint's got a point," Alice admitted. "Judge Hall wants to be sure this is a real commitment and that you didn't marry Clint just to adopt the baby, Jessie. So, you two don't have a thing to worry about, right?" she asked brightly.

"Right," Jessie agreed, forcing a bright smile. Clint leaned over and dropped a soft kiss on her frowning mouth. For Alice's sake, of course, Jessie reminded herself.

"See you later, Jess," he said with a secret smile. "We'll talk about all this at home, okay?"

"Okay." Jessie nodded. He turned to go, then suddenly looked back at her.

"What's for dinner?" he asked with obvious interest.

"You just had lunch," Jessie reminded him with a laugh. "Is food the only thing you think about lately, Clint?"

"Uh, no," he replied. His mouth twisted in a wicked grin as he caught her gaze with a simmering look that sent an unmistakably sexual message. "Not at all. I think about...a lot of things, Jessie. You know that."

Alice laughed into her coffee cup as Jessie blushed. Clint said goodbye once more and left the café.

That night at home, Jessie tried to talk strategy for their interview, but Clint wasn't very interested. Every time she brought the topic up, he would just tell her to relax and promise her that everything would go well.

Jessie dressed carefully for the meeting in a dark blue dress and black boots, with her hair pulled back in a low ponytail. Clint teased her when she came into the kitchen and claimed that he didn't know she was giving up the café to become head librarian.

"You'll never get hired though," he promised her. "You're too pretty. As Charlie would say, 'Folks won't like it. They'll be too distracted to read their books.'"

Jessie had to laugh at Clint's imitation of the cranky old cook. By the time they reached the courthouse, all of Clint's teasing had succeeded in taking her mind off her troubles. When the judge's clerk greeted them and led them into the judge's chambers, Jessie felt far more relaxed than she expected to feel. She sat in a chair in front of a huge mahogany desk and Clint sat beside her.

He reached over and squeezed her hand. "Don't worry," he whispered.

Just then the door opened and the judge entered. He was a tall thin man with thick white hair. He wore a dark gray three-piece suit with a navy blue bow tie, and had a pair of wire-rimmed glasses perched on his thin nose. He stepped up to them, shook their hands, smiling very briefly, Jessie noticed.

For the next half hour Jessie and Clint answered the judge's questions. And he had plenty of them. At first, they were mostly about their work and upbringing, why they wanted to be parents and the sorts of questions Jessie had already answered for Alice when she was interviewed to be Daisy's temporary guardian.

Then, just as Jessie had expected, he zeroed in on Jessie and Clint's relationship like a hawk swooping in for the kill. He paused and glanced down at an open file folder on his desk as he spoke.

"I think it's only fair to inform you, Mrs. Bradshaw, that the news had reached me a few weeks ago that this marriage was simply an arrangement of some kind, cooked up to increase your chances of winning custody of the child. And if that is the case," he said slowly, "I think it best that you and Mr. Bradshaw are frank with me at this point."

Jessie felt her blood run cold in her veins. She wanted to speak, but her words stuck in a lump at the back of her throat. Before she could reply, she felt Clint reach over and grip her hand.

"I can understand why you might be suspicious of us," Clint said suddenly. "And I will admit that when I proposed to Jessie, I knew she believed that getting married would help her win custody of Daisy. Maybe that wasn't fair or totally ethical. But frankly, I didn't see that I had much choice in the matter. If she was looking for a husband, I was determined to be that man."

"So she was looking for a husband and you volunteered, Mr. Bradshaw. Is that how it went?" Judge Hall asked pointedly. "Do you often volunteer to wed women in such need?"

"Judge, my usual style is to run like hell from a woman in need of a husband," Clint answered bluntly. "And at first, I thought Jessie was nothing but trouble in my life. But even I couldn't outrun my real feelings about this woman. The bottom line is," he added, "I fell in love with

Jessie the moment I first saw her. And I know now that whether I live the rest of my life with her, or without her, I will love her forever,'' he said simply.

Judge Hall gazed at Clint thoughtfully and tapped the folder on his desk with an expensive-looking gold pen. Jessie felt her pulse racing at Clint's words. Had he actually admitted that he loved her? From the first night they met? With her entire heart and soul, she wanted to believe that his admission had been true. But a more realistic voice reminded her that this was all playacting for the judge's sake.

"And what about you, Mrs. Bradshaw? Are you going to confess to me now that you, too, fell in love with your husband at first sight?" he asked in a cynical tone.

"Uh, no. Not at *first* sight, Your Honor." Jessie shook her head and ran the tip of her tongue over her parched lips. Clint still had hold of one of her hands and she could feel him staring at her, as well. "You see, when I first saw my husband, his head was bowed and he was covered with snow," Jessie explained to the Judge, "so I couldn't get a very good look at him—"

"And once he shook the snow off?" the judge cut in.

"Well . . . yes. I guess so. I guess it *was* right after he shook the snow off," Jessie said thoughtfully. "When I . . . looked into his eyes that first time, I think," she practically whispered, knowing full well that her words were true. "It's hard to pin these things down to the exact moment, of course," she added.

"Ah—yes. You looked into his eyes. Of course. I might have guessed that romantic twist," the judge echoed mockingly. "Then what happened, Mrs. Bradshaw?"

"Well, I was looking for a man to marry because I thought it would help with the adoption," she admitted. "But I never once imagined that Clint would want to marry me...." She felt Clint squeeze her hand, but she didn't dare look at him. "And when he first proposed," she added, "I said no."

"But you just said you loved him, Mrs. Bradshaw. Fell for him at *almost* first sight," the judge reminded her tersely. "What do you mean you said no?"

"I refused him because I thought it would be too difficult for me. Since I love him so much, I mean. And he didn't feel the same way about me," she explained.

"I see," the judge said. He stopped tapping his pen and tossed it aside. "But then you found out his true feelings for you, so you agreed. Is that how it all worked out?"

"Uh, yes." Jessie nodded. "We worked it all out...eventually."

She risked a glance at Clint. She had never seen quite such a look on his face before. He was staring at her as if two long purple antennae had sprouted out of her head.

The judge was silent for what seemed to Jessie a very long time. He stared down at the papers on his desk and jotted a note or two. He took off his glasses and wiped them with a clean white hankie, then slowly fitted them back on again.

"Quite a romantic tale," he said finally in his typically dry tone. Yet, there was something in his words, or in his eyes, that made Jessie feel he wasn't entirely untouched by their admissions.

Jessie noticed just then that the judge wore no wedding band, nor did he have any pictures of a wife or family around his office.

The judge coughed and cleared his throat. "Good luck in your marriage. I am satisfied that even though the timing was suspiciously convenient, this marriage is a true one." He glanced at Clint and then at Jessie. Then he straightened the papers on his desk and closed the file folder. "I guess that's all for this morning. Thank you both for coming to see me, Mr. and Mrs. Bradshaw. I have enjoyed our conversation."

Jessie left the chambers on wobbly legs. If Clint's strong arm hadn't been there to lean on, she knew she would have stumbled right into the courthouse hallway.

Neither of them spoke a word as they left the courthouse and climbed into Jessie's Jeep. Jessie started the engine.

Now is the time to tell him, a little voice prodded her. Just tell him that everything you said back there was true. He told the judge that he loved you, didn't he? Well, maybe he was telling the truth, too. Even if he wasn't, won't you be sorry if he never knows?

"I think it went well," he said finally. "I think the adoption is in the bag."

"Do you really think so?" she asked.

"No doubt in my mind," Clint replied. He glanced out his window, turning his face away from her view. "Then you'll have everything you ever wanted, Jessie."

Almost, Jessie wanted to say. For in his words she heard the unspoken acknowledgment that as soon as Daisy was adopted, their marriage deal would come to an end. Jessie took a deep breath and tried to concentrate on her driving. Yes, she was going to tell him that she loved him. Right now.

Right this minute.

"I guess we ought to get some sort of award for our wonderful performance back there," Clint said. "You were . . . very convincing," he added quietly.

"Excuse me?" Jessie had heard him and understood what he meant. She just needed a moment to collect herself.

"What we told the judge about...us," Clint explained. He glanced at her briefly, then stared out his window again. "Our acting job, right?"

She glanced at him and nodded. "Oh, right," she murmured.

"We laid it on a little thick at times, I thought. I was almost afraid he wasn't going to buy it. But I guess he's more of a sentimental old pushover than he wants to let on."

"I guess so," she agreed quietly.

Jessie felt as if she had driven head-on into a cement wall. Those sweet words she had longed to hear from Clint—those words she had heard him say—had only been pragmatic white lies, while she had been speaking her heart's truth.

She grabbed her sunglasses off the dashboard so that he couldn't see the tears gathering in her eyes. "Jessie, are you all right?" Clint asked.

"I, uh, just have a bad headache," she said curtly.

"You were just tense about the meeting," Clint said. "But it's over now and everything went fine." He reached across to her seat and massaged the back of her neck.

"Please don't do that," she said curtly. She pulled away from him.

"Oh, sorry. I thought it might help your headache. Your muscles do feel all tied in a knot." He sat back in his seat and glanced over at her.

"It's distracting me while I'm driving," she said. When in truth, it was hard to have him touch her in such a familiar way when she could no longer even pretend that he felt anything more than just sheer physical attraction for her.

"Do you want me to drive?" he asked solicitously.

"No, thanks. But I don't think I want to go to the café right now," she said. "I can drop you off there if you want to grab some lunch. I think I'd rather go home and spend some time with Daisy."

"Want me to come home with you? Daisy might be hard to handle if you have a bad headache. I'll just call the station and tell them I'll be in later this afternoon," he offered.

"There's no need to do that, Clint. You don't have to change your plans for me," Jessie replied. They had pulled into town and the café was in view. "Shall I drop you off at the café?" she asked him.

"Uh, sure." He nodded and grabbed his hat from the back seat. Jessie pulled up to the curb and stopped the car. "You're sure you're all right, Jessie?" he asked once more. He stared at her curiously.

"I'm fine," she insisted. I just fell off a big stupid cloud and took a crash landing on my head, she said silently.

"I'll call you later to see how you're doing," he said. He leaned toward her and Jessie thought he was going to kiss her on the cheek. She didn't move a muscle. She couldn't even turn her head to look at him. She was afraid that she might burst out crying.

He sat for a moment watching her. Then he opened the car door and got out.

Eight

Jessie spent the afternoon with Daisy and the charming baby girl provided the perfect distraction from Jessie's unhappiness. At five months old, Daisy was bright as a button and loved to play her favorite games with Jessie— peek-a-boo, clap-clap and find-the-pink-bunny, to name a few.

Every time Jessie looked at Daisy, she was reminded that the court date for the adoption hearing was drawing closer. Soon she would know for sure if she would win Daisy. It would mean the end of her marriage to Clint. But at least she'd have her little girl.

She was lucky that she hadn't poured her heart out to Clint today, she told herself again and again. He didn't love her. It was perfectly clear. He's never lied to you about his feelings, she reminded herself, and you're a fool to ever expect more.

At half-past four Clint called Jessie to see how she felt.
"I'm in town," he told her. "I can be home in a few minutes if you're not feeling well," he offered.

From her reaction to the sound of Clint's voice on the
phone line, she knew that she just wasn't ready to face him
yet. She was liable to spill the beans entirely, to humiliate
herself and make him feel uncomfortable . . . or worse.

"I, uh, feel fine. I was just getting ready to go out," she
stammered. "I thought I'd run up to the café and check
on things."

"Do you really have to go out? It's getting late."

"I have some bookkeeping to take care of and some
other work that really can't wait until tomorrow," she said
lightly. "Ivy will come over and sit with Daisy until you
get home."

"I'll wait to have dinner with you. What time will you
be back?" Clint asked.

"Oh, you go ahead without me. I'll get something at
the café," Jessie replied. "I won't be back too late."

Clint said goodbye and abruptly hung up. Jessie wondered if she was doing the right thing by avoiding him.
Maybe she should get it all out in the open, no matter
what the consequences. But she knew she wasn't ready for
that. Perhaps when it was time for him to go, she'd tell
him the truth. But not until then.

As soon as Jessie entered the café, Sophie left a table of
six customers who looked as if they were in the midst of
giving their order and ran straight over to meet her. From
the look on her face, Jessie guessed that she had some urgent news to deliver. Probably her side of the latest battle
with Charlie.

"Oh, Jessie—I'm glad you're here. I just called your
house to tell you, but you'd already left...." Sophie burst
out.

"I hope this isn't about another feud with Charlie," Jessie warned her. "You two are worse than children. Sometimes I think I should just fire the both of you," she said sternly.

"Jessie—what a way to talk," Sophie scoffed indignantly. It was clear that she wasn't a bit afraid that Jessie would actually follow through on the threat. They both knew that would never happen. "And my news has nothing to do whatsoever with that old coot in the kitchen. It's Sam Kincaid."

"Sam Kincaid?" Jessie asked. She hung up her coat and hat, then walked over to the register to check the daily receipts. "What about him?"

"He was in here, about half an hour ago, asking for you—that's what about him," Sophie said with satisfaction.

"Are you sure?" Jessie asked. Sam's family still lived in town, and she had heard through the grapevine from time to time that he had come to visit them. But in five long years he had never once called or stopped by the café to see her. Jessie thought that there must be some mistake.

"Wouldn't I know Sam Kincaid after all these years? I saw him grow up right under my nose," Sophie replied snappily. "Though I must say, he sure turned out a lot better looking than I would have predicted. He looked pretty well-off, wearing nice clothes and all. And he turned out to be a handsome devil. If you go for that smooth type, I mean."

So the city had agreed with Sam. Jessie might have expected he'd done well; he was so very determined to succeed when she knew him. She would have enjoyed seeing him after all these years, but she was suddenly glad that she'd missed his visit. She was in no mood tonight to put on a bright face for her old sweetheart. And hearing Sophie's description of his city sophistication, she suddenly felt very gauche and far too "country" in her red down vest, long denim skirt and boots.

"Well, sorry I missed him," Jessie said lightly. She closed the register and turned to the counter to fix herself some tea.

"Don't worry. He'll be back," Sophie assured her. "I told him you were coming in sometime tonight and he said he'd be back to see you."

"Oh, dear," Jessie mumbled under her breath. "Look, do me a favor, Sophie. When he comes, just tell him I'm not here, okay?"

"Sure, I'd do that for you," Sophie said agreeably. "Except it's too late." She glanced over at the café's large front window and Jessie followed her gaze.

A tall, blond man had just passed the window and was about to open the door. It was Sam. Jessie felt her heart skip a beat.

"He's seen you through the window already," Sophie concluded in a softer tone. "You still want to turn tail and run? Personally, I don't see as you've got anything to be ashamed of, Jessie," Sophie assured her.

"Thanks—" Jessie said weakly. She set the tea mug in her hand down on the counter. Her hands unconsciously smoothed her hair and then plucked at her butter yellow turtleneck sweater.

"Don't worry, honey," Sophie whispered. "He'll be plenty sorry when he gets a good look at you."

"Table number three wants to give their order, Sophie," Jessie gently reminded her. "Or do you plan to get it by mental telepathy?"

"I'm going, I'm going," she grumbled as she stalked off. "Just when things were getting lively around here, I get shooed off like an old house cat...."

The bells on the café door jingled and Sam Kincaid entered. Jessie saw his gaze move over the crowd of diners for an instant before it came to rest on her. He smiled, hesitantly at first, then wider as he walked calmly toward her.

Jessie felt a rush of a million emotions. It was Sam all right, and yet, it wasn't exactly the Sam she remembered. Maybe it was his expensive sport clothes, or simply the effects of time, Jessie reflected, but a certain awkwardness in his looks had been smoothed out. His long, lanky body had filled out and his entire manner reflected self-confidence, experience and maturity.

Sophie was right—he had turned out to be a handsome devil. And that fact was not lost on Jessie as he greeted her warmly. Not content to settle for a mere handshake, Sam leaned over and dropped a friendly kiss on her cheek.

"You look wonderful, Jessie," Sam said, taking her in from head to toe. "I heard that you just got married. It must agree with you."

"Is that what gave you the courage to face me after all these years, Sam?" Jessie asked lightly. "The news that I got married?"

"I know I deserve that...and worse," he said with his hands upraised in a gesture of apology. "Be honest. You still hate me, don't you?"

"I never hated you, Sam," she answered honestly. "Not for any longer than was therapeutically necessary, anyway," she joked. She crossed her arms over her chest and leaned back on the counter. "I did daydream a lot about running you over with Aunt Claire's truck at first. Nothing fatal, of course."

"Well, thanks. I appreciate that," he countered gracefully. As Sam made further apologies for his caddish behavior, Jessie sat back and observed the scene as if she were an objective third party.

It was amazingly easy to talk to him. Far easier than she'd ever imagined it could be. She wondered why that was—and then, she knew. She had no feelings for him. She didn't hate him, as she'd told him honestly. And she didn't love him, anymore either . . . not one tiny bit.

She felt warmly toward him, like some old school friend who she hadn't particularly missed in her life. And she felt suddenly quite proud of the achievement of getting past all her old painful baggage about this man.

They moved to a table, where Jessie joined him in a cup of coffee. She brought him up to date on her life—her aunt's retirement, her marriage to Clint and her plans to adopt Daisy. Then he brought her up to date on his life—his divorce, his disillusionment with city life and his interest in taking over his father's real-estate business as the elder Kincaid was planning to retire in the coming spring.

"Can you believe it?" he asked Jessie. "I once said I'd never come back to Hope Springs and now it looks like paradise to me. And the real-estate market around here is booming. It's a hot new spot for country homes."

Jessie had heard all about it and she'd certainly seen a lot more yuppies around town on the weekends. Personally, she hoped that the upwardly mobile would mobilize to some other hamlet for their weekend hideaways, and leave Hope Springs as unspoiled and unfashionable as always.

"Does that mean I have to get a cappuccino machine in here?" she asked. "Charlie and Sophie are liable to blow the place up. . . ."

"You always made me laugh, Jessie," he said warmly. "I always loved that about you." He reached over and quite unexpectedly squeezed her hand.

Jessie stared down at Sam's once-familiar hand covering hers. It was an awkward moment.

Made even more awkward by the unexpected sight of Clint, who suddenly appeared beside the table. Jessie looked up at her husband and snatched her hand from Sam's grasp, nearly knocking her coffee cup over in the process.

"Clint...I—I didn't see you come in," Jessie stammered.

"Obviously," he said grimly. His face was a dark expressionless mask. His blue-gray eyes looked the color of tornado clouds. Jessie did her best to ignore the storm warnings she read there.

"Clint—I'd like you to meet an old...uh, friend of mine," she continued. "This is Sam Kincaid. Sam, this is my husband, Clint."

"Pleased to meet you, Clint." Sam stood up and offered his hand. Although he was smiling, Jessie could see him taking inventory of Clint. "Jessie's told me a lot about you."

"And I've heard all about you," Clint replied. He did not smile, but politely shook Sam's hand. Maybe a bit too firmly, Jessie noted, as she saw the younger man stifle a wince of pain.

Without asking for an invitation, Clint sat down in a seat between Jessie and Sam.

"Hey, don't let me cut your visit short," he said. "I think I'll have some coffee, too."

He signaled to Sophie, who instantly arrived with a mug of coffee for him. She tried to linger to listen in on the

conversation, but Jessie's glare chased her away. Clint and
Sam simply stared at each other with forced smiles.

They were like two stallions, kicking the dirt and tossing their heads, squaring off in the corral, she thought
wryly. She might have been flattered, except she was realistic enough to know that all this snorting and snuffing
had very little to do with her. It was a male thing—pure
and simple. Men were so funny sometimes.

"So what brings you to town, Sam?" Clint asked with
forced politeness. "Just stop by for a stroll down memory lane with my wife? Nice of you to come before you
both turned senile," he added.

"Sam is thinking about moving back to Hope Springs,"
Jessie cut in. "His father is retiring and Sam might take
over the real-estate brokerage."

"Is that right?" Clint said with interest. "You mean,
Kincaid Realty, right across the street?"

"That's the place," Sam said proudly. "My father
opened that office over thirty years ago."

"But I thought you were in business in the city. What
happened? Couldn't make a go of it?" he asked inno-
cently.

"Well—" Sam hedged. "Not as well as I expected, I
suppose. It's not like Hope Springs. It's a lot more com-
petitive out there, you know," he added in a somewhat
condescending tone, Jessie thought.

"Couldn't take it, huh?" Clint asked bluntly.

"That's not what I meant, but—" Sam stammered.

"Oh, I think I know what you meant," Clint replied
easily. "You're just looking for an 'easier life-style,' as
they say," Clint said derisively. "You'll have your father's business handed to you on a platter—all the hard
work done there. Then you'll make some easy deals with
the local hayseeds. Isn't that it?" Clint said, still smiling.

"Clint—" Jessie said nervously.

"What's the matter, honey? Did I say something wrong?"

"Gee—I didn't realize the time," Sam said, glancing at his watch. "My parents are expecting me."

"Oh—sure," Jessie said, relieved to see him go. "Say hello for me, will you?"

"Sure thing," Sam said with a smile. "They always loved you, Jessie." He looked at her for a long moment, then turned to Clint. "Good to meet you, Clint," he added as he buttoned up his coat. "By the way, you're a very lucky man."

"I know," Clint said gruffly.

"See you around," Sam said as he left them.

Once Sam had gone, Jessie turned to Clint. What in the world had come over him? If she hadn't known better, she would have said he was jealous. But of course, he could still feel possessive of her, even if he didn't actually love her, she reflected. She was still, at least in name, his wife.

"You weren't very polite to him, Clint," Jessie said lightly.

"That's funny. I thought you could have been a hell of a lot ruder. Why, after what he did to you, you're just sitting here, having a damn tea party," he growled at her. "If I were you, I would have just shown that skunk the door."

"I didn't mind talking to him after all these years," Jessie said with a light shrug. "I think he just came to apologize. Since he's planning on moving back to town, I mean. He probably expected me to make some horrible scene and he wanted to get it over with."

"I don't see why that guy has to move back here. Who wants him anyway?" Clint grumbled. He glanced up at Jessie. "I bet you won't like having him in here every day, drinking coffee and trying to swindle his way back into everyone's heart.''

''Oh, it won't be so bad,'' she said honestly.

''It won't?'' Clint said curiously. ''I would think that you'd have stronger feelings about the man, Jessie. Considering what he did to you. But he just shows up here, says he's sorry and you're all ready to forgive and forget.''

Yes, it did sound rather wimpy of her when Clint explained it that way. But it was impossible to explain her feelings to him.

''Well, maybe it's time to forgive and forget,'' she replied thoughtfully. ''Maybe it's time for me to just let go of the past.'' She looked up at him.

He stared back at her with a brooding expression on his handsome face. The face she loved so very much.

You changed my life and that's why everything looks different to me now, she wanted so much to say. But she couldn't. She picked up her coffee cup and took a sip.

She knew now that Sam had been her childhood sweetheart and she had loved him in an immature way. Her marriage to Clint showed her what love between a man and woman really was, and those wonderful feelings had enabled her to finally let go of the past.

''I'm going home,'' Clint said abruptly as he came to his feet. ''Are you coming?''

''In a little while,'' Jessie said. ''I still have to take care of some—''

''Yes, I know, *bookkeeping,*'' he said harshly. ''Let's just hope no more of your old beaus show up tonight, or you'll never get to finish it.''

He flipped up the collar of his coat and walked away from her before she could answer.

* * *

It finally happened—Jessie was legally and officially Daisy's mother. The hearing took place as scheduled, about two weeks after the private meeting with Judge Hall. Jessie was so tense, she could hardly keep her attention focused on what was being said. First her lawyer spoke and then Alice and then some other representative from the social services department. Sitting on his bench in his black robes, Judge Hall looked even more sour and formidable than he had in his chambers the day of their interview. He asked Jessie and Clint a few questions—Jessie nervously answered, unsure of even her own name at that point.

Finally he spoke, granting Jessie and Clint's adoption of Daisy. Jessie sat immobilized beside Clint in the courtroom, feeling completely stunned. She couldn't believe it was over, and she and Clint had won. Judge Hall adjourned the court, then rose from his chair and exited the courtroom.

She heard Alice's voice beside her, and her gleeful words of congratulations. She felt Clint's arm around her, holding her close, yet she barely responded.

"Jessie—we won," Clint whispered in her hair. "We won, thank God. We won," he repeated.

"Is it really over?" she asked them both. "Daisy is ours?"

"She's all yours, Jessie," Alice said.

"God, I just can't believe it—" Jessie shook her head. She hadn't even realized that she was crying until Clint brought it to her attention.

"Don't cry, Jess—" Clint handed her his handkerchief and she wiped her eyes. "Oh, hell—cry if you want to. I guess you deserve a good long cry after what you've been through."

She looked at him and had to laugh. "I'm sorry...I don't mean to be such a waterworks..."

"It's okay," he whispered back. "Everything is perfect now, right?"

She sniffed and smiled at him through her tears. Then she remembered. No, it wasn't perfect. She had only traded off one heart's desire for another, for now that Daisy's adoption was finalized, her deal with Clint was coming to an end. There was no reason for them to remain married and the deadline that they had agreed upon had arrived.

"Hey, what are we sitting around here for anyway?" Clint asked the two women. "Let's go get that little girl and celebrate."

Jessie happily agreed and promised herself that she would at the very least enjoy this day. Hand in hand, they quickly left the courthouse and headed for the café, where Ivy and Sophie were baby-sitting Daisy. When Jessie, Clint and Alice arrived, they found a party of well-wishers, eager to celebrate Daisy's adoption.

Charlie had even baked a cake that said Happy Adoption Darling Daisy across the top in pink swirling letters.

As soon as Jessie entered the café, Ivy handed Daisy into Jessie's arms. "Here's your mommy, honey," Sophie said with tears in her eyes.

With a cheerful cry, Daisy hugged her and tugged her hair. "Oh, my sweet girl." Jessie laughed, holding her close. "I missed you."

Clint stepped close and put his arms around the both of them. "It's wonderful, isn't it? She's really your girl now, Jessie. No one can ever take her away."

She reached up and touched his cheek, then on tiptoes, she kissed him. "Thank you," she whispered. "Thank you for helping me. I couldn't have done it without you."

"You don't need to thank me, Jessie. I did it because I—" His voice faltered. "I'm just glad everything worked out. You've got everything you wanted now, don't you?" he said finally.

Jessie couldn't answer him. She loved Daisy with all her heart and being Daisy's mother was an answer to a prayer. How did she dare ask for more? Jessie wondered. You can only expect so much from life, Aunt Claire had always taught her. And perhaps, to wish for Clint's love, too, was simply asking too much.

Nine

Clint left the house at sunrise. He didn't need to start work quite so early, but lately he'd had trouble sleeping. Trouble sleeping beside Jessie and not daring to touch her. He'd left her this morning with the quilt tucked up to her chin and her golden red hair fanned out on the pillow. She looked to him like a cherished dream—a dream he knew now would never come true.

After Daisy's adoption became final, Clint had decided to give Jessie two weeks. It had seemed a reasonable amount of time for her to give him some sign that she wanted him to stay. But as of today those two weeks were over and still Jessie had not sounded a word on the subject either way.

After the hearing he thought she would say something about his leaving. But she didn't. That was a good sign, he thought at first. A very good sign, since in his darker moments he was certain that she'd married him only to win custody of the little girl.

But things just hadn't been the same between them. Not since the adoption was made final—maybe not even since their meeting with the judge, Clint calculated when he looked back. Clint couldn't quite understand it. When she had told the judge that she loved him, his heart had filled with hope—a slim hope that she had come to feel something for him. Enough hope for him to put aside his haunting fear of losing everything if he even dared to let himself love again.

He'd been just about ready to tell her everything—how much he loved her and needed her and Daisy in his life, though he had once believed he could never feel that way again.

But he'd never gotten the chance to say it. He'd tested the waters and found that he'd been mistaken. Jessie had only been acting a part for the honorable Judge Hall. She'd said as much herself, hadn't she? He knew going in that she'd be willing to say anything to win Daisy. To sell her very soul, if necessary. Clint forced himself to face the cruel, cold truth. The way he saw it now, once she'd been reasonably sure that the judge would rule in their favor, she had withdrawn from him. From that very first afternoon on.

Things changed. She didn't want to be around him anymore. She made excuses to be out when he was home. There was always some convenient emergency at the café. And at night, she was tired—not just tired, exhausted. She'd practically fall into her plate at the dinner table and be asleep before her head even hit the pillow. As much as he wanted to make love to her, he wasn't about to force himself on her. He still had some pride. And she was moody. She'd burst into tears at the drop of hat. The other night, when he suggested she see a doctor to find out why she was so tired all the time, she just burst out in tears. The woman was just plain unhappy. He couldn't lie to himself any longer. She didn't want to be married to him anymore, but Jessie, being the sweet wonderful woman she was, didn't know how to tell him. He couldn't account for it any other way.

Then there was that damn Sam Kincaid. Every time Clint stopped by the café these days, there was Sam. Didn't the man ever do any work? Didn't he have anything better to do than sit around eating doughnuts and trying to seduce another guy's wife?

Jessie was still in love with Kincaid. The thought was like a white-hot dagger in his heart, but Clint couldn't turn away from the possibility. Maybe that visit wasn't a surprise. Maybe she'd known all along he was coming to town. Maybe Kincaid had called or written to her and Jessie had never told him. If she didn't still love him, then why was she so damn nice to a guy who had been such a bastard to her?

She had Daisy now, Clint thought. That was the only reason she had married him. And now Jessie was probably just waiting for him to disappear so that she could be reunited with her long-lost true love. Well, he'd make it easier for her. He'd tell her that it was time he moved on. He'd done her the favor she needed and now he was free to go. He'd do it. He'd do it today.

As Clint drove through town, headed for the station house, he considered his future. It seemed mighty blank and bleak without Jessie and Daisy in his life.

Well, a man had to make his plans. A man had to carry on. He'd decided he'd leave town, find a new job someplace far from Hope Springs. How could he hang around and see Jessie with another man? Simple answer—he couldn't do it. He'd seen a notice posted on the office bulletin board about a job opening in Woodstock. He'd look into it. He'd always liked a change of scene. Hell, in a month or two, he wouldn't even remember what she looked like, Clint told himself. Though he knew in his heart that wasn't true.

No, what he had told Judge Hall was the God's honest truth—with her, or without her, he'd love Jessie for the rest of his life.

Jessie checked the calendar in her date book, carefully counting the days. She was late. Very late. No doubt about it. She had expected her period right about the time of the hearing. With all the stress, she hadn't wondered when it didn't arrive on schedule. Her body had never been that reliable that way. Besides, there was no reason to worry about being pregnant, she reminded herself—she and Clint used protection every time they'd made love.

But two weeks had passed and even she couldn't ignore the signs that she was possibly pregnant. The other night, she had just burst into tears when Clint casually suggested that she see a doctor to find out why she was so tired lately.

Hormones, no doubt. And anxiety.

The idea of having Clint's child was both thrilling and terrifying to her. Terrifying when she tried to figure out how to break the news to Clint if it was in fact true.

Everything was just so...unsettled between them. And in light of his past, she didn't expect that he would be thrilled to hear she was expecting his child. He would probably feel exactly the opposite.

Jessie heard Daisy on the baby monitor, stirring in her crib as she woke up from her morning nap. Jessie jumped up from her chair and felt suddenly dizzy and sick to her

stomach. She barely made it to the bathroom before she
lost her breakfast.

Afterward, she sat on the edge of the bathtub and
cleaned her face with a cold washrag. It was time for a
home-pregnancy test. She had find out for sure. And then
she had to find some way to tell Clint.

Later that morning, Jessie bundled up Daisy and drove
to a mall miles outside of town to buy her pregnancy test.
She knew that if she purchased the item in the drugstore
on Main Street, Ida Lewis would have the news around
town before Jessie had even read the instructions.

When Daisy went down for a nap in the afternoon and
everyone else was busy with the lunch rush, Jessie snuck
into the rest room.

The dot turned blue.

She stared at, feeling as if she was about to faint. She
had bought two tests, just in case, and tried the second
one. Same result.

Jessie hid the evidence and staggered into Daisy's away-
from-home nursery. Jessie still had her desk set up there
and she dropped down into her chair and put her head
down on the desk. She didn't know whether to sing with
joy, or weep with unhappiness. She felt like doing both—
simultaneously.

But it was clearly time to get back to work. Sophie and
Charlie were at it again, and from the sound, it was time
for her to step in as referee. Jessie rose and walked quickly
into the kitchen, where she found Charlie and Sophie in
their usual belligerent poses. Sophie stood with one hand
on an ample hip and the other wielding a large squeeze
bottle of mustard. Charlie had a cream pie in hand and
was waving it around rather ominously. Although they
had never come to actual physical blows, they did enjoy
pretending each time they very well might.

"All right, you two. Just cool down," Jessie said, standing between them with her hands raised like a traffic cop. She turned to look each of them in the eye. "I don't know what it's about this time, but you're going to wake the baby with all this—"

Jessie stopped talking and shook her head. The dizziness again. Only, this time it was worse. The room was spinning and she had to hold on to the edge of the big oak chopping block to get her balance.

"Jessie? What's going on?" Charlie rushed to her side. He reached her just in time to support her before she sagged to the floor.

"Oh my lord!" Sophie cried out as she ran to help. She knelt down beside Jessie and supported her head. "Can you hear me, Jess? Just nod if you can hear me," she said. Then to Charlie she said, "I think she's fainted. Get the smelling salts in the first-aid box. Call Ivy in here. Get some help...."

When Clint neared the house in the late afternoon, he was surprised to see a car in the driveway. He hadn't expected Jessie to be home; she was supposed to be at the café. But it wasn't Jessie's Jeep he noticed as he pulled into the driveway. It was a flashy red BMW with personalized plates that read SK-I-BUM. Then he recognized it—Kincaid's Yuppie mobile.

He felt as if the top of his head were going to blow right off. Was he about to interrupt some little afternoon love tryst? He would have given Jessie more credit than that; he would have thought she'd have enough decency to at least wait until he was out of the picture.

His first impulse was to just gun the engine and head back on the road. But he stopped himself. No, it would be easier this way, he decided. It was going to turn his stomach to walk in there and find them together. But if it had to end like this, so much the better. Besides, this would give him a damn good excuse to land one big fat solid punch on Kincaid's despicable kisser.

With any luck, Clint reflected as he tramped up to the front door, he'd at least bust the guy's nose.

Clint was about to put his key in the door, when it swung open. Sam Kincaid stood in the doorway. Clint glared at him.

"Good—you're here," Sam greeted him with relief. "Jessie didn't want to call you, but I guess Sophie reached you after we left...."

"Left where? I haven't spoken to Sophie." Clint entered the house. He looked around for Jessie. But she was nowhere to be seen. "Where's my wife?" he demanded.

"I just left her up in the bedroom—"

Clint gulped. He felt the blood pounding in his head. Instinctively, his hand closed in a fist and his arm moved back as he wound up for a knockout punch. "Helped her into bed, did you?" he echoed. "Why you son of a—"

"Whoa there—" Sam saw the punch coming and deftly moved out of the way. He quickly ducked behind the coat tree as Clint succeeded in socking one of Jessie's wide-brimmed hats clear into the living room.

"W-wait a second, pal," Sam stammered as the hat sailed past his head. "It's not what you thi—"

"I'm not your pal, Kincaid. In case you didn't notice," Clint clarified as he ominously moved in on the coat tree again.

"Jessie is sick. She fainted at the café and she wouldn't let anyone call you," Sam explained in a rush. "I happened to be there and I offered to drive her home."

"Jessie fainted?" Clint paused. Without wasting a further glance at Sam, he ran up the stairs two at a time to the bedroom. As he reached the bedroom door, he heard the front door close. Sam had made a quick exit, he realized. At least the man knew how to save his own hide. Because if he opened this door and found out he'd been fed a cock-and-bull story...

Clint slowly opened the bedroom door. Jessie rested fully clothed on the bed. She had dark circles under her eyes and her skin looked as pale as the white pillowcase behind her head, he noticed.

"Jessie?" Clint whispered her name and her eyes fluttered open.

"Oh, dear...I didn't want you to see me like this, Clint...." She sighed and tried to sit up, but he could see that it was a struggle. He instantly came to her side and sat at the edge of the bed.

"You just lay back now and rest. Let me call the doctor. I'll take you over there right now." He pressed his hand to her forehead. Her skin felt cool. "You don't feel as if you have a fever. Maybe it's something you ate."

"It's not something I ate," Jessie assured him. She slowly sat up and tried to gather her strength. "I'll be fine in a minute, if I just can get up and—"

"Now just a second." Clint put both hands on her shoulders so that she couldn't get off the bed. "You're sick, Jessie. You look like hell—"

"Thanks a bunch," she said weakly.

"Well, I'm sorry, but you do," he insisted. "You haven't been yourself for weeks and now Kincaid tells me you fainted at the café. Is that true?" he demanded to know.

"I'm okay. I just got a little dizzy," she fibbed. "Now, just let me up, Clint."

"No. I'm taking you to the doctor," he said firmly.

"I don't need a doctor," she argued back at him.

"We'll see about that," he said. "For crying out loud, Jessie. I wish you would just stop being so damn contrary for five minutes, and let me take of you. I am still your husband, you know."

He stared into her eyes. His face was close to hers; she could have leaned over and kissed him with no trouble at all. How she wanted to.

"How long?" she asked him.

"What do you mean?" he quietly replied.

"I mean how long do you plan on being my husband?" she asked bluntly.

"How long do you want me to be?" he replied, his expression turning as grimly serious as she'd ever imagined it could look.

"As long as you want to," she said slowly.

He leaned back, but took one of her hands and held it in both of his own. "I thought maybe you wanted me to make way for Sam Kincaid," he said quietly. "I thought maybe, now that the adoption is final and there's no reason for us to stay married, you wanted me to—"

"Sam Kincaid?" Jessie sat bolt upright. "What in the world ever gave you that crazy idea?"

"Well . . . you were in love with him once. You told me yourself," Clint said. "Look, I wouldn't blame you if you were still in love with him."

"I don't want Sam Kincaid," Jessie said, bounding off the bed. She stood in front of Clint and stared at him in utter disbelief. "I want *you,* you big loon! I love you with all my heart and soul. Can't you tell?"

"You do? Really?" Clint rose off the bed and put his arms around her. "I just thought—oh, heck. Never mind what I thought. I had it all wrong. All mixed-up in my stupid head." He hugged her so tightly, she could barely breathe. "Jessie, I love you so much. Every word I told that judge was the God's honest truth, but I didn't dare tell you. I was such a damn coward. I thought, from what you said afterward, that you were just making it all up to get Daisy."

Jessie pulled back her head and looked up at him. "I thought *you* had just made it all up."

"So you really fell in love with me the first time you looked in my eyes?" he asked her in a teasing tone.

"Yes, I think so," she confessed. "Of course, I didn't realize it then. I didn't realize it for a while. Not until you proposed to me, I think."

"And that's why you didn't want to marry me? Because you loved me?" he asked in a puzzled tone.

"It made perfect sense to me at the time," Jessie said indignantly. "Though I must say, I'm glad it worked out differently."

"I love you, Jessie. I love you with all my heart," Clint said, pulling her close. He brushed back her hair with his hand and then their lips met in a deep, soul-wrenching kiss.

Jessie felt dizzy again. Dizzy with unimaginable joy. She answered her husband's deep, soulful kiss, imagining the loving pleasures they would soon share.

Then she pulled away from him, suddenly aware that her stomach demanded immediate attention. Mumbling an unintelligible excuse, she pushed Clint aside and dashed into the bathroom.

Clint ran after her, stopping short as she slammed the bathroom door in his face.

"Jessie? Are you all right in there?" he demanded. "I'm going to call a doctor right now...."

"I'll be right out," she managed to call back.

He waited restlessly until she emerged from the bathroom. He rushed to her side to help her over to the bed.

"Honey, I've rarely told a woman that I loved her. But I didn't think it was supposed to cause quite that reaction," he quipped. "Are you *sure* you're not sick?"

"Clint—sit down." Jessie pulled his hand so that he was sitting next to her on the bed. "I'm pregnant," she said simply.

She watched his face. He blinked. He took hold of her shoulders in his hands. "Say that again," he demanded.

She couldn't tell if he was happy or disappointed at the news. She bit down on her lower lip. "I said that I'm—"

"I heard what you said," he cut in. "But we were so careful—"

"Well, something must have slipped or broken or misfired...." She shrugged. "Then there was that time in the shower," she recalled wistfully.

"Oh, yeah...." His eyes widened as he recalled the night. "The shower... Oh, Jessie. We're really going to—" His words caught in his throat as he pulled her close and pressed his face in her hair. "I love you so much. A baby... Why am I such a lucky son of a—" Clint's final words were muffled against Jessie's lips as he kissed her deeply.

Assured that he felt as happy about the news as she did, Jessie kissed her husband again and again. They fell to the bed, entwined in a passionate embrace, and before too long, their clothes were scattered in every direction and their bodies joined as one.

After the lovemaking, Jessie lay with her head resting on Clint's bare chest. Clint rested his hand on her bare belly, touching her with tender reverence.

"So when is this new baby coming?" he asked her happily.

"About next December, I guess. Daisy will have a little sister or brother, God willing," Jessie replied.

"Good timing, darling," Clint said firmly, hugging Jessie close again. "I think we should start a family tradition. From now on in, every Christmas, we'll get ourselves a new baby. What do you say?"

"I love you so," she answered. "You're the best thing that ever happened to me. Next to Daisy, of course."

"And you are the best thing that ever happened to me," he said softly as he stared into her eyes. "And you and Daisy and our new baby are more than I could ever hope for."

Jessie closed her eyes and kissed him. It was the only way she could reply. As she imagined the future and the life she would share with the man she loved and their children, her heart was so full of joy, there were no words to describe her happiness.

*   *   *   *   *

SILHOUETTE
Desire

COMING NEXT MONTH

WHO'S THE BOSS? Barbara Boswell

Man of the Month

When masterful Cade Austin inherited 49% of a company and Kylie Brennan was heir to the other 51%, Cade planned to buy her out and send her on her way. Instead, he found he was battling it out—in the boardroom *and* the bedroom!

RESOLVED TO (RE)MARRY Carole Buck

Holiday Honeymoons

When thieves broke in to Lucy Falco's office on New Year's Eve, she was stunned when she was tied up with her ex-husband, Chris Banks! It wasn't long before they discovered how steamy their passion still was...

THE YOU-CAN'T-MAKE-ME BRIDE Leanne Banks

How To Catch a Princess

Remembering his wickedly handsome grin, Jenna Jean knew that former bad boy Stan Michaels was *not* husband material. Stan thought otherwise, but there was only one woman the confirmed bachelor considered *was* wife material—Jenna Jean!

GEORGIA MEETS HER GROOM Elizabeth Bevarly

The Family McCormick

Georgia Lavender had thought Jack McCormick would always be around to protect her from her father—then Jack disappeared. Now, finally, he'd returned to rescue her—and found she'd turned into a beautiful, sophisticated woman. Now *he* was the one in danger!

PRACTICE HUSBAND Judith McWilliams

Joe Barrington was not a marrying man. But when Joe found himself teaching his friend Addy Edson how to attract a husband, would Addy's practice kisses lure him to the altar?

THE BABY BLIZZARD Caroline Cross

Loner Jack Sheridan enjoyed his solitary life until a snowstorm stranded him with expectant mother Tess Danielson. Now he was forced to look after Tess and her new baby until the snow—or his heart—thawed.

COMING NEXT MONTH FROM

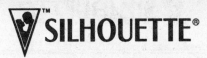

Sensation

*A thrilling mix of passion, adventure
and drama*

MUMMY BY SURPRISE Paula Detmer Riggs
THE BADDEST VIRGIN IN TEXAS Maggie Shayne
TEARS OF THE SHAMAN Rebecca Daniels
HAPPY NEW YEAR—BABY! Marie Ferrarella

Intrigue

Danger, deception and desire

HOTSHOT P.I. B. J. Daniels
WED TO A STRANGER Jule McBride
THUNDER MOUNTAIN Rachel Lee
LULLABY DECEPTION Susan Kearney

Special Edition

Satisfying romances packed with emotion

HUSBAND BY THE HOUR Susan Mallery
COWBOY'S LADY Victoria Pade
REMEMBER ME? Jennifer Mikels
MARRIAGE MATERIAL Ruth Wind
RINGS, ROSES...AND ROMANCE Barbara Benedict
A DOCTOR IN THE HOUSE Ellen Tanner Marsh

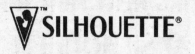

FREE!

FOUR FREE
specially selected
Desire™ novels
PLUS a Mystery Gift
when you return this page...

Return this coupon and we'll send you 4 Silhouette® romances from the Desire series and a mystery gift absolutely FREE! We'll even pay the postage and packing for you.

We're making you this offer to introduce you to the benefits of the Reader Service™– FREE home delivery of brand-new Silhouette novels, at least a month before they are available in the shops, FREE gifts and a monthly Newsletter packed with information, competitions, author pages and lots more...

Accepting these FREE books and gift places you under no obligation to buy, you may cancel at any time, even after receiving just your free shipment. Simply complete the coupon below and send it to:

THE READER SERVICE, FREEPOST, CROYDON, SURREY, CR9 3WZ.

EIRE READERS PLEASE SEND COUPON TO: P.O. BOX 4546, DUBLIN 24.

NO STAMP NEEDED

Yes, please send me 4 free Silhouette Desire novels and a mystery gift. I understand that unless you hear from me, I will receive 6 superb new titles every month for just £2.40* each, postage and packing free. I am under no obligation to purchase any books and I may cancel or suspend my subscription at any time, but the free books and gift will be mine to keep in any case.

(I am over 18 years of age)

D7YE

Ms/Mrs/Miss/Mr ....INITIALS ....

BLOCK CAPITALS PLEASE

SURNAME..

ADDRESS..

....

....POSTCODE...............................

Offer not valid to current Reader Service subscribers. We reserve the right to refuse an application and applicants must be aged 18 years or over. Only one application per household. Terms and prices subject to change without notice. Offer expires 30th June 1998. You may be mailed with offers from reputable companies as a result of this application. If you would prefer not to receive such offers, please tick this box. ☐

Silhouette® is a registered trademark of Harlequin Enterprises used under licence by Harlequin Mills & Boon Limited.

New York Times **Bestselling Author**

REBECCA BRANDEWYNE

Glory Seekers

Broadcast journalist Claire Connelly is reunited with
her ex-lover, homicide detective Jake Seringo, as they
both investigate the death of a US senator's wife.
Up against corruption, lies and murder, they race to
untangle a web of secrets that could topple a dynasty.

*"Like fine wines, some writers seem to get better and
better. Rebecca Brandewyne belongs to this vintage
group"*—**Romantic Times**

1-55166-276-0
AVAILABLE FROM DECEMBER 1997

Barbara
DELINSKY

THE DREAM

She'd do anything to save her family home.

Jessica Crosslyn was prepared for the challenge of saving
her family's home—but she wasn't prepared to share the
project with Carter Malloy, a man she loathed. They
could work together to restore the house, but mending
past mistakes proved to be more difficult.

*"When you care to read the very best, the name of
Barbara Delinsky should come immediately to
mind."*—Rave Reviews

1-55166-061-X
AVAILABLE FROM DECEMBER 1997

MIRA®

GET TO KNOW

THE BEST OF ENEMIES

the latest blockbuster from TAYLOR SMITH

Who would you trust with your life? Think again.

Linked to a terrorist bombing, a young student goes missing. One woman believes in the girl's innocence and is determined to find her before she is silenced. Leya Nash has to decide—quickly—who to trust. The wrong choice could be fatal.

—

Valid only in the UK & Ireland against purchases made in retail outlets and not in conjunction with any Reader Service or other offer.

50ᵖ OFF

COUPON

VALID UNTIL: 28.2.1998

TAYLOR SMITH'S *THE BEST OF ENEMIES*

9 904170 200509 >

0472 00189